THE POWDER MONKEY

A 1798 STORY

BILL WALL

MERCIER PRESS

BY THE SAME AUTHOR

The Slave Coast
a sequel to *The Powder Monkey*

Published in 1996 by Mercier Press
PO Box 5 5 French Church Street Cork
Tel: (021) 275040; Fax: (021) 274969
e.mail: books@mercier.ie
16 Hume Street Dublin 2
Tel: (01) 661 5299; Fax: (01) 661 8583
e.mail: books@marino.ie

Trade enquiries to CMD Distribution
55A Spruce Avenue
Stillorgan Industrial Park
Blackrock County Dublin
Tel: (01) 294 2556; Fax: (01) 294 2564

© Bill Wall 1996

ISBN 1 85635 154 8
10 9 8 7 6 5 4
A CIP record for this title is available
from the British Library

Cover: Penhouse Design Group
Set by Richard Parfrey
Printed in Ireland by ColourBooks
Baldoyle Industrial Estate, Dublin 13

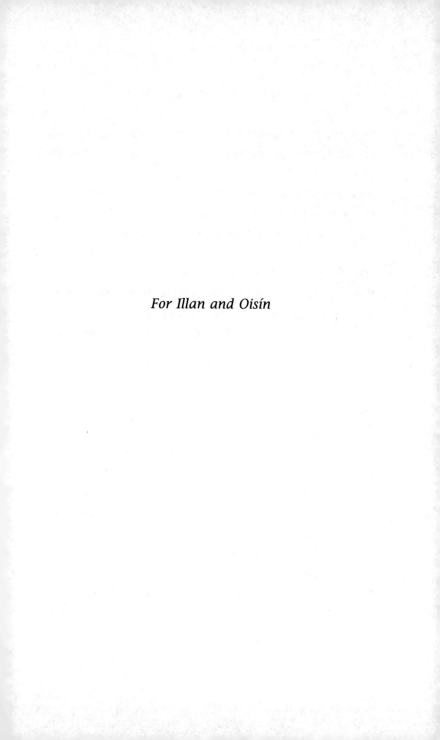

For Illan and Oisín

CONTENTS

1	Poison	7
2	The *Ellen Brice*	22
3	Roundshot	33
4	The Topgallant	44
5	Murder!	59
6	The French are on the Sea	73
7	The Enemy Landed	86
8	Encounter with a Spy	96
9	'All Hands to Witness Punishment'	109
10	A Yeoman Colonel	119
11	The Prison Van	129
12	Mr Wilson's Bargain	141
13	Last Days on the *Leander*	152

1
—

POISON

Dónal was shivering, although it was a summer's night and not a very cold one. It was close to the time when his uncle would come home from Sheehan's drinking-house and he knew what would happen then.

His uncle would stumble in, cursing the darkness and kicking the stool or whatever was in his way. Then he would look for the stirabout.

It was Dónal's duty to make stirabout every evening before dark, so that when his uncle came back from his drinking there would be something for him to eat. But the stirabout got cold and thick and his uncle hated that. Dónal would hear the rattle of the spoon in the stirabout pot. The sound his uncle made eating always seemed unnaturally loud in the darkness. Then Dónal would hear him cursing the cold porridge and the clinking sound of the belt being unbuckled, and after that the stinging pain of the leather lashing his face or his legs or his back through the thin blanket.

This did not happen all the time because Michael Long sometimes did not have the money to drink. Then he was a decent man, quiet and well-mannered. He would work steadily for weeks on end, keeping his own garden of potatoes or going out with the fishermen when the mackerel were in or working for the Tates or the Furneys who had the big farms nearby. They knew him well and knew he was a hard worker. They would pay him so many shillings each week and Dónal would see the shiny shillings going into a leather bag that his uncle kept hidden behind a stone in the wall. He was civil to Dónal then, too. There would be potatoes and buttermilk on the table and sometimes even the salt fish that reminded Dónal of his father. They might sit outside the cabin on summer evenings and watch the boats returning to the bay below them, or listen to the bells of Furneys' cows as they made their way back from the milking.

At times like this Dónal would feel close to his uncle and able to pity him for his drinking, which was like a disease that broke out in him as soon as the little bag of shillings began to bulge. Michael Long could not keep money; everyone said that. While the shillings were going into the bag he would talk about buying a passage to America for the two of them, or buying a farm in the better land to the east, or buying a boat of his own from the boatyards across the harbour as Dónal's father had done, or marrying one or other of the strong farmers' daughters whom he had his eye on. In the end, though, he was like the small glowing embers that hid under the ash of the fire. In the morning you would think to look at the grey ash that the fire was dead but if you stirred the ash the embers would be there and by blowing gently across them you could coax the fire into life again. Then, like his uncle when the shillings were in the bag, the fire would blaze up. Merry at first and full of warmth and light, later it would be the hard hot glow that spat sparks on the cabin floor.

When Michael Long felt those shillings mounting he would take out the bag and with a face full of shame tell Dónal that he was going out for a bit. Dónal knew he would be gone for the night. He would come back merry and full of talk, but the talk now would be of the great things he had done or said in Sheehan's shebeen, the songs he sang and bargains he had made. He liked to talk then of joining the United Irishmen, and how the French would put a musket in the hands of every loyal Irishman, how they would march on Cork and drive the tyrants out. Ireland would be theirs and the French would aid them.

Dónal knew very well that the United Men would not let his uncle swear the secret oath that would make him a member because they did not want a drunkard who could not hold his tongue.

Dónal's father had been a United Man but he and Michael Long were as different as two brothers could be. Dónal's father had owned one of the new sailing hookers that were being built near Kinsale and he was one of the best captains in the harbour. All the men wanted to sail with him but he always took the same three men, all sworn members of the brotherhood. All of them could read and sometimes on calm nights when the nets had been shot and there was nothing to do but wait, they would discuss the latest news from France or some book that they had found. They were always talking about *liberty* and *the rights of man*, and names of men like Wolfe

Tone and Lord Edward and Grattan were tossed about as if they were familiar friends.

But his father never talked just for the sake of it. He paid a penny a day for Dónal to go to the one-legged master who kept a school in the parlour of a nearby farmhouse. Dónal learned Latin, Greek and Mathematics, and his father promised him that if he stuck to his books the master would teach him navigation because he had been to sea for a time in the Royal Navy. He had lost his leg fighting the Portuguese. The hope of learning navigation kept Dónal at school. He longed for the day he could stand on the deck of his father's boat as a fisherman, not as the captain's son. When his father took him out fishing all the men made jokes for him or told him funny stories. They treated him as a kind of pet. They would not let him do the work that any boy could do on a boat because he was the captain's son. But one day he would buy a boat like his father's and together they would chase the shoals and shoot their nets on the moonlit nights. Dónal longed for that day.

Dónal liked the one-legged schoolmaster but the other boys made fun of him because he had fought for England. His father didn't approve of this and he patiently explained what Wolfe Tone, founder of the United Irishmen had said, and Dónal remembered the words because his father repeated them often: 'To unite the whole people of Ireland, to abolish the memory of past dissensions, to substitute the common name of Irishman . . . '

'The truth is, Dónal,' his father often said, 'that we spend too much time fighting among ourselves.'

When Dónal was ten the world had fallen apart. First

there was the crop failure of 1794. A bad summer caused the potatoes to fail. The corn was not much better, the ears eaten by mildew in the constant damp. Typhoid fever came to the village, the same fever that had taken Dónal's mother when he was still a baby. Within weeks it had swept through the village and some of the outlying farms. People were hungry and the fever raged through their weakened bodies. Dónal's father had died in the same bed that Dónal slept in now. His boat lay idle on the mud. One of his crew died too. Another set off to walk to Cork in the hope of finding work and was never heard of again.

After Dónal's father was buried, his uncle Michael moved in. At first he was sober and worked hard. Together, he and Dónal and the last crewman tried to work the boat, constantly at sea in cold misty misery, but the mackerel were slow to come in that year and this meant there was very little money. In the end the boat was taken from them to pay their debts. Michael Long was not a sailor anyway, and Dónal, though he could not say so, knew more about fishing than he did.

That was when Dónal saw his uncle's first drinking bout. He laughed in the early days at the wonderful stories his uncle could spin when he was merry. His uncle dreamed about making a new life in America, about buying one of those New England boats that they heard about, of fishing the Grand Banks. Or he dreamed about buying land in the Carolinas and seeing the wild men who lived in the wilderness. But when the fire of his drinking was burning down, the dark hour came upon Michael Long and he became a tyrant. After the first beating Dónal knew his life would hang on a thread until the money ran out and the drinking ended. For the first time in his life, Dónal was terrified.

Dónal had learned patience from his father, who taught him that at sea everyone must wait – for the gale to die down, for the breeze to give a fair set for the fishing ground, for the fish to fill the nets, for the tide to turn. So when Dónal thought of a plan he was patient. It took him a year to decide to do it and two years to prepare it, even though it was a simple plan.

His father's boat still lay rotting in the mud of the bay because the fever and the bad harvests had taken so many men that there weren't even enough crewmen for the boats whose captains were still alive. This was the same all round the harbour. In Cove a man could walk on to a boat and get a place even if he had never fished before. Many of the Crosshaven boats were idle. An experienced fisherman could name his own pay, it was said, and many were getting shares in boats who had never owned a thing before in their lives. Boats whose skippers had died were lying idle all round the harbour, from Raffeen Creek to Guileen. Sometimes one came up for auction and could be bought for a fraction of its true price. Mostly they were left to sit on the mud, waiting for the price to rise.

Dónal's plan was to steal his father's boat and sail it to America. He knew it would be hard but it could be done because he and his father had often worked the boat alone. He would not worry about a fast crossing, but would keep the sails reefed in all but the quietest weather. Every night he would reef the sails down so that if a wind or high sea sprang up he would not have to take chances. It would take him months, and food and water would be the biggest problem, but he knew he could fish and catch rainwater, and he would take with him enough potatoes to last him as food. He would leave in June when the potatoes were about to be harvested and steal whatever he could from his uncle's garden, the rest from his neighbours. For a time he even considered taking his uncle's goat for the milk, but changed his mind when he remembered that he would have to feed her as well. Besides, she was a terror for eating things. One night he dreamed he was asleep on the deck of his father's boat and the goat was eating the sails.

So for two years he had watched the boat, dreading that it would be taken from him, that some fisherman would come from across the harbour, his pockets full of gold sovereigns, and Dónal would see him standing on the deck and trying the tiller and stamping on the timbers to see if they were sound.

But no one came. Every day the tide came in and lifted her and she creaked out of her mud bed, her mooring lines came tight and her mast stood up. When she lay in the mud she had a sad look about her, down-at-heel and forlorn. But when the tide rustled in and filled around her she began to come alive. When she stood bravely at the top of the tide Dónal sometimes felt that his father's proud spirit had taken hold of her helm, that his father's heart was her heart. She was the *Ellen Brice*. That was his mother's name before they were married. It seemed to him the perfect name for a boat. When he had his own boat in Nantucket or in the Newfoundland fisheries, he would call her *Ellen Brice*.

So he plotted and schemed. He scoured the seashore

for anything that might prove useful. Pieces of net cut away from some hapless fishing smack in a storm, a length of good hempen rope, a wooden barrel, a tarry jacket with one sleeve missing but still good enough to keep out the rain, a wooden fid for splicing ropes: all these things were given to him by the sea. He begged, borrowed or stole many other things. His father's knife was his by right. He took it from his uncle while he lay drunk and snoring. He stole the waxed thread needed to mend sails and hid it with the other things in a cave along the seashore. He begged scraps of sailcloth from the men working on the pier.

None of these things were easy to find. It was a triumph for Dónal when he found a scrap of rope washed up among the rocks after a storm. It was a triumph when he found the jacket with the sleeve missing because it was a sailor's tarpaulin jacket and he knew that not even the fishermen had jackets like that. In those days, although the boat captains were better off than the tenant farmers, they were still poor and their lives were hard.

Dónal knew that if he were caught stealing, he could be tried in the Assize Court and his sentence might be transportation. Transportation meant being taken to Australia to work as a slave for the length of your sentence. In some ways it was worse than prison or a flogging. Dónal took great care not to be caught, but every time something came his way a shiver of fear ran down his spine.

He was worried too, about stealing from his neighbours and his uncle. His father had taught him that stealing was always wrong but that stealing from his own people was doubly wrong because they were so poor. When he stole the potatoes, the food that his neighbours relied upon, he told himself he would take only a few from each family, so that they would hardly notice it. He told himself that he would one day pay them back, if he lived.

At last it was June of 1798 and the time came to put his plan into action.

In that terrible year the country seemed to have gone mad. There were stories that all of Wexford had risen in open rebellion, thousands of people taking to the hills, fighting the muskets and cannon of the army with pikes and swords. General Lake, it was said, had marched on Ulster with an army of militia and yeomanry, and had burned and tortured wherever he went. By early June, people fleeing the fighting had spread the news that the rebels had been successful. They had defeated the North Cork militia and captured Enniscorthy and Wexford Town itself. Wolfe Tone was in France and the new French government was promising to send soldiers to aid the United Irishmen. People were beginning to cut their hair short in the French fashion.

But there was bad news too. Edward Fitzgerald, the man everyone thought would be president of the new republic that would follow the rebellion, had been shot and died of his wounds in prison. The brothers Sheares, young Thomas Emmet and Oliver Bond had all been arrested on the word of a spy.

The trouble was everywhere. Fourteen men from Dónal's village of Ballymonas had been taken up and tried at the Cork Assizes for being members of the United Irishmen, for being traitors to the King. Eight of them were in fact United Men, the rest were innocent fishermen and farmers. They now lay in Cork Gaol with a sentence of hanging on them. There were daily and nightly horseback patrols travelling the country and it was dangerous even to be out after dark. People had been horsewhipped by the patrols for coming home late from a shebeen. John Whelan the blacksmith, who had pulled Dónal's bad tooth a week before, had been tortured, and his daughters had had their hair shorn. Terrible stories spread from other parts of the country, of people being killed in their beds, of floggings and hangings. Many of the United Irishmen had gone into hiding but many more were afraid to leave their homes in case it would draw attention to them and perhaps lead to the arrest of their families. No one felt safe.

Only Dónal was happy.

He knew his escape was close at hand. He knew it was only a matter of time before he had the helm of the *Ellen Brice* in his hands, before he felt the roll of the sea under his feet. All that was needed was to keep his uncle out of the way, long enough to work the boat out of the harbour on the falling tide.

Dónal had planned that too.

For two months in the early spring Dónal had worked in the house of Old Furney, a kindly man who tried to help his poorer tenants. He had got a job helping the cook and the gardener. It had enabled him to save a few precious pennies and to hide them in his cave, and also to steal a large quantity of salt. Not wanting to keep the salt in the cave where it might soak up the dampness of the sea water, he had hidden it between the rafters and the thatched roof of his cabin. Up there it was snug and dry in its cloth sack. When his uncle was away he would take it down and dry it even more near the fire. He took as much care of that bag of salt as if it were a bag of gold or jewels.

Now Dónal was shivering in his bed, shivering out of fear, expecting to hear his uncle's steps on the boreen at any moment.

Earlier in the evening, when the time came to make the stirabout porridge for his uncle, Dónal had carefully mixed the oatmeal, the water and the salt. As the water went in, Dónal tipped in more and more of the salt from his bag.

He spent a long time making sure that the stirabout would be smooth. Then, instead of trying to sleep as he normally did, he sat there tending the stirabout pot until he knew that the time of his uncle's return was approaching. Tonight for sure his uncle would not find the stirabout in the pot cold or lumpy but warm and smooth and pleasing to his whiskey-burned throat. Dónal guessed that his uncle's mouth would be so inflamed by the illegal whiskey that they sold in Sheehan's shebeen, that he would not taste the salt. Or the taste might even be pleasing. He had often heard men say that they craved salt bacon after drinking. But the salty stirabout would make his uncle very thirsty and Dónal, whose job it was to draw water from the well to the house, had taken care to spill out the water after he made the stirabout. The well was almost a mile away across the fields.

Dónal heard his uncle stumbling over the dusty boreen that led from the main road. He sang as he walked and with a thrill of horror Dónal realised that the song he was singing was enough to have him hanged, if a company of yeomen were passing on patrol. Even though he was going to leave his uncle, he was furious that in these inflamed times Michael Long should put himself and his nephew in danger simply because he could not keep silent, because whiskey was his true king. What if Michael Long were taken? How many others would go to the gallows with him? Michael Long would surely talk under torture. Even the threat of torture would be enough to make that drunkard and bully tell the Yeomen everything they needed to know. Hot tears ran down Dónal's face, tears of anger and sorrow and frustration. Anger that his father had died of the fever and his uncle had lived. Anger that his uncle wasted every penny he earned. Anger because his uncle wasn't half the man his father was. Anger at the world that was so cruel and had taken Dónal's father and mother and other good people and had left the wicked and the wasteful.

He heard the door opening, then his uncle struggling to remove his greatcoat. Muttering quietly to himself, his uncle hunkered down by the fire and tasted the stirabout.

Dónal was frozen with fear now, scarcely capable of shivering in case the sound was heard. He held his breath until he thought he would burst.

The spoon clanked in the pot again. His uncle was taking a second spoonful. This time Dónal heard an approving murmur. Now the spoon clattered regularly. He could hear his uncle talking quietly to himself about how Dónal had finally learned how to make the real thing, complimenting himself on having taught his nephew well, declaring to God that the stuff was good.

Now Dónal could hardly keep from laughing. It was working. His uncle was stuffing the porridge down. Shortly, Dónal heard the spoon scraping the bottom of the pot. His uncle had finished the whole pot of stirabout.

Dónal crept from his bed as soon as Michael Long was snoring. He found his uncle's boots by the slight glow of the fire and, reaching up over the fireplace, he hung them by their laces to a hook high up in the sooty chimney. His uncle would never think to look up there. He dressed himself and climbed back into bed again to wait for the explosion.

As the young moon was rising above Hadwell Hill, Dónal heard a change in his uncle's breathing. He was no longer snoring but muttering loudly in a dream and licking his lips. Several times Dónal heard the word 'water'.

He must have dozed off because he awoke from a pleasant dream to see his uncle lunging about in the moonlight looking for his boots.

'What ails you, uncle?'

'No water, Dónal lad. Not a drop. Oh, God, water. I'm killed with the thirst. Mike Sheehan must have poisoned the whiskey on me. Go down to the well for water, for God's sake. No. I'll have to go meself. Where's me boots? Rise up and find me boots for me. I have to go down to the well for water.'

Dónal got up but stayed in the shadows so that his clothes would not be noticed. He pretended to search, aware all the time that his uncle's searching was becoming more and more frantic. The stool was knocked across the floor, the bed was lifted and thrown on its side. The butter box that they kept the oatmeal in was tipped over, the oatmeal spreading across the mud floor of the cabin like a dusting of snow. Now he was searching blindly near the fire. The stirabout pot went clattering off its hook and his uncle cried out in pain as it came down on his toe. It was the pot that pushed him over the edge. He bellowed with rage and pain, threw the door open and set off across the fields in the direction of the well, in his bare feet. The last words Dónal heard him say were: 'God, God, the poisoned whiskey.'

In the pale moonlight Dónal gathered the things he had hidden in the cave, and stowed them carefully in a small boat he was borrowing for the purpose. Once he had everything aboard he would leave the borrowed boat on the *Ellen Brice*'s mooring. He rowed all the bits and pieces out – the sacks of potatoes, the sailcloth, the rope, the netting, the fid, the barrel of water, the tarry jacket and more besides. When he had everything aboard he tied the borrowed boat to the mooring ropes and cast off. He felt the *Ellen Brice* turning slowly on the tide. Soon she was drifting down the bay, pulled by the ebb and pushed by a gentle night breeze. Somewhere in the distance he imagined he could hear his uncle, still blind drunk and roaring with the thirst. In that state it could take him hours to find the well, and when he got there he would find that Dónal had filled it with sand from the seashore so that it would not be possible to drink from it until the sand had been scooped out. By then, in fact, it would scarcely matter anyway, because the *Ellen Brice* would have cleared the harbour and her bowsprit would be faced towards America.

He went below and hauled the staysail up on deck. It was tattered and dirty but it was a sail. He got it tied on and hauled it up the mast. It billowed gently on the breeze like a coat lifting in the wind. It was the work of a moment to sheet it home. The wind filled it out into the proper rounded shape and he felt the boat come alive slowly under his feet. Once clear of Ballymonas Bay and out into the wider harbour he would set the other sails. In an hour he would be at sea. He went back and took the tiller in his hands, pushing it this way and that to try the steering. The *Ellen Brice* had been sitting too long in the mud berth and her bottom was clogged with weeds but she still answered the helm. She would steer. She would sail.

He was free.

2

THE *ELLEN BRICE*

The sun warmed Dónal as he stood at the helm. The *Ellen Brice* was leaning over in the light dawn breeze and he could hear the water chuckling against the planks. She was a sight to see under sail. All her sails were dark red and they looked like huge wings above him now. Dónal remembered the pleasure his father used to take in hearing him name the sails, and just for his father's sake he named them now to himself. He cast his eye from one to the other as he did so, and watched the way the wind ruffled them. He was happy for a time, and he called out the sails' names to the passing waves. The names were like magic to him, the magic language he spoke in his boyhood. Soon he set to remembering the names of each rope and piece of wood as well. He even knew some of the names in Irish because one of his father's men spoke Irish and taught him the soft names that made his father laugh. Then his eye went out to the sea and fear gripped his heart again.

There was a long high swell driving up from the south which lifted the *Ellen Brice* high up and then plunged her down into a deep trough. A landsman might be frightened by this swell just because it seemed as if the waves were very big, but Dónal knew better than that. Such swells are caused by faraway storms and the waves can travel hundreds of miles from the storm itself. Perhaps the storm had blown itself out a thousand miles away, half-way to America. Or perhaps it had weakened so that it was no more than a puff that would not even fill the sails.

But what if the storm were coming, in all its fury? Sometimes a swell like that foretold a terrible wind. It would be a big storm to make such high swells, Dónal thought, so he hoped to be far from land before it came.

The landsman always thinks that the sailor is safest closer to shore, but Dónal's father had taught him that a boat is far safer out to sea when the wind blows high. Out on the sea there is only the wind, the sea and the boat to worry about. Close to the land a boat is in much greater danger from the land itself. So now Dónal hoped, by breaking his own rule and setting as much sail as he dared, to get clear of the land before the storm came. He had set all the ordinary sails the boat could carry, leaving out the topsail and the squaresail. These were awkward to handle and he wasn't even sure he knew how to set them.

There was another problem that worried him. As soon as he got out of Cork Harbour he had lashed the helm and let the boat sail herself, as all good fishing boats are required to do, and he had gone below to stow his gear. The noise down there was frightening at first as the boat rose and plunged in the swell. He soon became accust-omed to it, but as he worked at sorting the mess of gear his father had left below, a new sound forced itself into his mind, the sound of water swirling about in the space below the floorboards. There is always water in this area, the bilge. But to Dónal's ears there seemed to be an awful lot of it. He lifted a loose board and looked down into the wet darkness below. Black water was swirling beneath him, only a few inches from his face.

Since then he had gone down several times and each time the water was a little higher. He knew that the planks the boat is made of can dry out in warm weather, and when the boat goes to sea she takes up a lot of water at first. Then the planks swell and close up the gaps and the water stops coming in. He hoped this was the problem. In the meantime he tried the old pump that was fitted in the waist of the boat. It should have pumped water out over the side and emptied the boat quite quickly, but when he pumped it hard for what seemed like a long time, all that came out was a trickle of grey muddy water. He guessed that the pump had become clogged with mud. He would have to free that before the storm came.

He could still see the coast of Ireland, low down on the horizon behind him. The falling tide had at first carried him to the west so that he was not far from Kinsale. Now he was drifting more slowly eastwards. He could see the sails of some fishing smacks in the distance and the square sails of big ships coming and going to Cork. He had brought oatmeal with him and put some to soak in buttermilk for an hour. Now he swallowed it down, glad of something to fill his belly, despite the coarse watery taste. He laughed as he ate, to think of his uncle desperately searching for the well and cursing Sheehan's poisoned whiskey!

'That's for all the beatings you gave me!' he shouted at the sky, and laughed aloud.

He wondered how long he would have to sail in his southerly course. At first, he knew, he had to sail away from land. If he passed too close to another fishing boat someone would recognise the *Ellen Brice*. They would come alongside and ask about the captain and when no captain could be found to answer them they would come aboard and take his boat from him. Or if he passed a merchant ship or a man-of-war, they would launch a boat to investigate. Then the game would be up.

His sole aim at the moment was to get clear of the fishing grounds inshore, to clear the shipping lanes where the coastal boats went east and west and head for the open sea. Then the time would come when he would swing the boat around and point her face at the setting sun. He would follow that sun until, in weeks or months, he would see it setting behind the coast of North America. No one he knew had ever done such a daring thing but in his heart he knew he could do it.

By evening the sky had filled with cloud and the wind was blowing hard from the southwest. Dónal had taken off most of the sail. Only a scrap of red cloth flew at the forestay now, and another scrap clung to the mast and boom. These were the *Ellen Brice*'s storm sails, to give a crew enough control to keep her going in the storm.

Dónal checked the ropes on these sails a dozen times before he was happy. He knew that if the wind was too strong, not even the sails would hold, but it was a comfort to go over his work and be sure of it. He coiled away any loose rope and tied the hatches down as he had seen his father do.

The water had been rising in the bilge and at times it lapped over the floorboards. Dónal had put everything that might suffer from the dampness into his father's locker where it would be safe. He had tried to reach the base of the pump to clear the blockage, but his hands would not reach that far, and down there the smell was so bad that it made him feel seasick. He must not get sick because then he would not be able to fight the boat through the storm.

He came back on deck and put on his tarry jacket, realising for the first time how small and thin it was in comparison to the great sweeps of white water that were rushing towards him.

He took the length of hempen rope he had found among the rocks at home and tied a special knot, a double bowline, into it. He slipped it around his waist. Then he tied the other end as a lifeline to the post where the nets were tied on. This was one of the strongest parts of the boat. If a wave washed over the deck and dragged him into the sea, he would be still tied to the boat and he might be able to haul himself back aboard. Lastly he took a shorter length of rope and looped it around himself and the tiller.

The *Ellen Brice* was becoming difficult to steer. He guessed that the weight of water in the bilges was making her heavy and there was three years of weed on her bottom to slow her down. A slow boat is not easy to control.

The waves were coming at him from the side and more than once the boat was heeled right over so that he found himself slipping down to stand against the side rail and looking directly down at the boiling water. Whenever that happened he lost his grip on the tiller and the boat's head began to turn towards the waves. If he did not get her under control she would round up into the wind and he would be at the mercy of the sea.

Then the rain came.

Even in the darkness he could see it coming towards him, a black sheet from the sky to the sea, and at its base was a line of white where the rain and wind whipped the water into a frenzy. A squall, he thought. Then, remembering a squall that had struck years ago when he was fishing with his father, and which had almost destroyed the sails, he twisted out of his short loop and raced for the mast. He must get some of the sail off.

The lifeline stopped him within three feet of the mast, and without a thought he turned to cut it, reaching to his belt for his father's knife. It was too late. The rain and wind were on him, like a wild animal wrestling him to the ground. The boat heaved over on to her side and his feet slipped from under him. He crashed across the deck and came to rest against the bulwarks. His feet were in water and he realised that all this side of the boat was underwater. The *Ellen Brice* was straining herself beyond breaking point. Over the roar of the wind and sea he heard an explosive crack and saw the storm jib break free at one corner, a huge rip along its foot. Within seconds it flapped itself into ribbons. Now, with some pressure off, the boat came more upright and Dónal was able to scramble back to his place at the tiller.

Within a few hours the situation had gone from bad to worse. Complete darkness was on him now and darkness at sea can be a frightening thing in itself. There were none of the comforting signs to look for that there would have been on land. Wherever he turned there was only blackness, not so much as a pinprick of light. But most frightening of all was the roaring of breaking waves and the whiteness of the crests as they toppled on to the boat.

The *Ellen Brice* was rushing along like a runaway horse, plunging from crest to crest. There was a loud screaming in the rigging and water seemed to be exploding under the bow. How long can I go on like this? he thought. How long can the boat stand it? His heart was seized with exultation, a kind of fierce, defiant pride. He was master of his own vessel! He was riding a storm to America! He would never see his uncle again. His father would be proud of his seamanship and courage. He could almost hear his father's voice in the wind shouting: 'Good lad, Dónal! There's my lad!'

Two hours later the wind was screaming at him that he would die of cold if he didn't drown. The seas were still huge and they seemed to be coming from every direction now. Occasionally a wave would wash clean over the boat, immersing him in icy blackness while he clung on for his life: then all of a sudden another wave, from a different direction, would surge along the top of the gunwale and force him backwards as if he would go over the stern. Every second wave broke over the boat and drenched him.

He was tired and cold and hungry. He was frightened

too, because he knew by the feel of the boat that she was settling. The water in her hold must be getting higher but he couldn't leave the tiller to look, much less to try to pump it out. He knew that if he left his post, the boat would topple into the sea and they would both be lost. He was beginning to feel that his strength was the only thing that kept the storm at bay, that his hands held the boat together. He felt that, as he weakened, the *Ellen Brice* was slowly sinking, and in his exhaustion he began to talk to the boat as if she could understand him.

'You saved my father many a time,' he told her. 'Now why wouldn't you save me? Amn't I the captain now? My father always said if I was ever in trouble on the sea I only had to put my trust in you and you would be the saving of me.' Although his talk did not change the wind or the sea, it gave him comfort and he found the courage to go on.

All through the night he stayed at the helm, blinded by wind and spray and driving rain. The pain of the cold on his hands and face was so bad that he thought he was dying. After a time he found that he could not take his hands off the helm because his fingers would not open. Nor could he stretch his elbows. He was locked on to that piece of timber by his own exhausted muscles.

He thought at times that he was asleep because he had strange dreams.

Once he saw a huge bird with white wings as big as sails going by in front of him. It had a beak as long as a rowing boat and its tail had a sharp point.

Once he saw his father quietly coiling down a rope in the bow. When Dónal called out to him he vanished and he woke to find himself in the same frozen misery as before.

Once he was at home by the fire swirling the spoon in his uncle's stirabout.

Once he was sitting behind a man on horseback, his arms clasped tightly around the rider's waist. He spoke to this man and when he turned his face towards him, Dónal realised that the man was a yeoman and he, Dónal, was under arrest as a traitor. He struggled but could not escape from the horse.

All these dreams came to him in the fury of the storm. He was no longer steering now, just holding the tiller. He kept his eyes closed mostly, because they hurt so much. Several times he prayed that the sea would either take him or calm down. He didn't know whether he wanted to live or die.

In time the rain stopped and a watery sunrise warmed his back. This was his second sunrise at sea, but now it shone upon a world of chaos. Everywhere he looked Dónal saw white water, waves curling and breaking in every direction. The second sail had blown apart during the night and the boat was now wallowing in the troughs. She had settled lower still and was close to sinking completely by now. He must pump. He remembered the sailors' song he had often heard: *It's pump or drown boys, pump or drown.*

The pump gushed slime and water, a bucketful with every pump of the handle. The rising water must have freed the pipe. Dónal pumped for his life, up down, up down. If he could get the water level down, she would sail again and he might live after all.

He pumped until his arms were too weak to pump any more, then he crawled to the hatch and looked down at his fear.

Below decks everything was awash. The water was up to the level of his father's bunk. All his pumping could only have made a few inches of difference. Through his fear and exhaustion he realised that the *Ellen Brice* was not going to save him this time. She would sink out here and he would go with her, because even though he could swim, he was too tired to bother.

He crawled back to the tiller and waited.

The storm was a short and vicious one, and after such storms the sea sometimes settles quickly. The waves were slowly getting smaller. The wind was light, the sky was clear and the sun was warm. With no sails up and the hold full of water, the *Ellen Brice* was more like a raft than a boat.

Dónal fell asleep where he lay, curled up by the tiller on the open deck. He dreamed another strange dream. He heard voices which he knew were on his boat. He wanted to shout to them to go away, that he would have no pirates on his boat, but no sound would come. He dreamed he heard them talking about the *Ellen Brice* and saying she was sure to founder, and asking where was all her crew?

Suddenly, it came to him that one of the voices was his father's and the other was that of his father's crewman who had also died of the fever. Now he could relax, he thought. His father had come back to steer the boat to safety. They would make sail and pump her out, and in a few days he would be in the New World.

They picked him up and lowered him into a boat and after that the last thing he heard was someone shouting 'Boat ahoy'.

3

—

ROUNDSHOT

The crew had loaded the gun with powder and shot. Best, the gun captain, gave his orders softly and they ran the gun out through the port and stood back. He sighted along the barrel and made some changes to the angle, then pricked the powder bag, pushed in the quill and poured the loose powder from his primer into the priming hole. He straightened up and cocked the flintlock.

'Gun ready, sir,' he said to Lieutenant Tobias Wilson, the officer who stood behind him.

'Very well, Best. Fire when you are ready.'

The gun captain took one last look down the muzzle, stepped back and pulled the lanyard. A huge explosion followed as the gun jumped back on its tackle. Smoke filled the space in front of the gun port and drifted around the lower gun deck.

Looking past the gun, Lieutenant Wilson followed the flight of the ball, saw it rise slightly then begin the slow curve downwards, saw it smash into the little fishing smack that was drifting with its sails blown out, scarcely far enough out of the water to say that it was afloat. The huge thirty-two pound ball smashed through the boat's sides, opening a great hole in the timbers. The officer could imagine its journey down through the lower deck and out through the rotten timbers at the bilge. Another great hole would be opened in the bottom of the boat because no fishing boat had strong enough timbers to resist a thirty-two pounder. His guess was confirmed when he saw the boat settle evenly into the water until only her topmast was showing. Soon, even that was gone. By then the order had been given to make sail. Men were heaving at the yards to brace them into the wind, others were lying out on the yards and letting the sails fall, men were heaving in the sheets on the bow, while a shantyman sang a song about some naval victory in days gone by to encourage the work.

To a stranger, the deck of a man-of-war in the process of making sail was a perfect picture of chaos, but in reality every man knew his job and every job was perfectly timed and organised. This was Captain Henry Coyle Somerville's ship, and she was trim and fast. Her mission was to cruise east and west along the coast of Ireland in case the French tried to land, and to engage any enemy ship that was sighted, and since Captain Somerville was an Irishman who passed his own home every week or so on this cruise, everything aboard was done to perfection, even to the point of firing a gun every time they passed his home in daylight. Needless to say Tobias Wilson had his work cut out for him, with a perfectionist as his captain, and this being his first serious posting. Twice already they had entertained friends and relations of Captain Somerville and he had almost fallen in love with a certain Miss Halpin who had come aboard on the last occasion. He was hopeful that sooner or later they would see some action because action meant prize money, and with prize money he could hope to impress Miss Halpin.

Master Gunner Best, who had seen his shot strike home with his usual satisfaction, had a low opinion of Tobias Wilson and a high opinion of Captain Somerville, on whose ships he had served for the past six years. Captain Somerville was a hard-driving captain, but he was a fair one, and above all he was a brave one. On the three occasions they had sighted the enemy, Somerville had given chase. Once they had captured a French frigate and when the prize money had been paid out on that, Best had invested it in his brother's tavern in Portsmouth. One or two more of those, he told himself, and he could go ashore and sit by a warm fire for the rest of his days. No more turning out at all hours of the night, in all weathers, to make or shorten sail. No more saucy bosun to drive him to his work with a kick or a blow. Master Gunner Best looked forward to their next action because it would mean money in his pocket.

Captain Somerville stood on his quarterdeck on the upwind side.

Lieutenant Wilson saluted and said, 'Reporting the fishing smack sunk, sir.'

'Very good, Mr Wilson,' said Captain Somerville. 'We will cruise eastwards as before. I doubt not but the French will attempt a landing. Let us pray we come upon them.'

'Yes sir.'

'What do you make of the smack, Mr Wilson?'

'A funny business, sir. Typical of the Irish.'

Captain Somerville stared at him and Wilson remembered yet again that this man *was* an Irishman. 'Crew lost, I should think, sir. In last night's gale, I should think. Timbers rotten through and through, sir. Best saw them. Reported the boat full of water, sir. I'm surprised she stood up to last night at all. '

Captain Somerville turned away. He did not much like Tobias Wilson.

'Well, we shall see, no doubt. Put a man in the foretop, as usual. Tell him to keep a sharp lookout and sing out for any sail. Any sail, I say.'

Wilson turned away, aware that yet again he had irritated his captain. Irritating captains was not something young lieutenants should do.

The creak of the rigging, the squeaking of the numerous wooden blocks and tarred ropes, the timbers of the hull, the sounds of sailors' voices as they worked, the barked orders of the officer of the watch or the bosun, the steady hissing of the sea beyond the planks – Dónal wondered if he was at last in heaven as his mind came back from the deepest sleep he had ever had. He was amazed to find that he was warm and lying on straw. By his head was what looked like a wheel and above that some sort of black metal object. Beyond that again was a clean white ceiling with an oil lantern swinging from it. He tried to sit up and found himself very weak, but the movement brought people to him. He stared up into the faces of three men whom he had never seen before in his life.

'Where am I, at all?'

'*Leander*, mate. Ship o' the line, king's navy.'

'We took you off t'smack, matey.'

'Saved your bleedin' useless neck.'

They seemed to find this very funny and laughed loudly.

'Be you Irish?' the second one asked.

Dónal replied that he was.

'There's Irish on the *Leander*. How'd you get into that state? On the smack? Where's the crew gone?'

'You didn't eat 'em, did you mate?'

Dónal asked for water and they laughed. One of them went off and the others kept smiling down at him and winking at each other. They talked constantly, too, telling him how many guns the ship carried, that her captain was a decent old man, that they were bound to fight the French – and anything else that came into their heads. When the third man returned, Dónal sat up and drank from the mug he was offered. He knew immediately that it was some kind of spirit because his uncle had often played that trick on him, making him drink whiskey when he thought it was water. It burned his throat and made his eyes stream but he swallowed some of it and handed back the mug, thanking them.

They stared at him for a moment before breaking out into howls of laughter, slapping each other on the back and shaking Dónal's hand. He had behaved correctly, it seemed. By swallowing some of the liquor he had made friends with them.

Now a fourth man appeared, pushing the others aside. Dónal thought he recognised the voice of the man from his dream. The accent was Irish but with a hint of sailor's English about it.

'Stand aside there,' he said. 'Captain's orders.'

'He be an Irish, Charlie Madden. One o' your watch. Talk to him, matey.'

"E can take his tot of rum, I'll say that much.'

'Matter o'fact, he's drunk as a lord!'

Charlie Madden brushed them aside and stood before Dónal. 'It was me picked you off your smack,' he said. 'Only for me you were dead.'

Dónal thanked him.

'No need to say that, mate. You'd do the same for me. Can you walk?' Dónal nodded his head. 'Right. Captain wants to talk to you.' He reached out a hand and Dónal took it and at once felt the power that was in that grip. It was a gentle grip and did not hurt him. Dónal staggered to his feet and found that he had been lying beside a huge gun. On his other side was a plain wooden table with wooden buckets on it. Beneath his feet were the oak timbers of a warship, and over his head the huge beams that held up the deck above. A warm breeze came through the opened gun ports and evening sunlight slanted across the floor.

Madden marched him along the deck and Dónal saw to his right and left the neat rows of guns that told him he was indeed on a warship. As they marched and climbed the steps to the next deck, Madden told him his whole life story in short bursts.

'Father was a shopkeeper near the Cove of Cork. I was press-ganged in '88. Nearly went mad the first year at being forced into it. Got used to it. Joined the *Leander* four years ago. Good captain, the old man is. Likes the Irish. Irish himself. Bit of bad luck in the last action.' He

showed Dónal his left hand and Dónal saw that two
fingers were missing. 'Round shot. Lucky it didn't hit me
fair and square. Surgeon took one off. Never found the
other one. Here we are.'

Captain Somerville was a small pale man, who looked
even smaller in the huge day cabin. He sat behind a desk
that almost hid him and looked Dónal up and down.
Dónal was a tall thin boy, bearing obvious signs of
hardship – the dirty grey face, the sunken eyes, the thin,
almost transparent skin. Yet this boy had survived a
vicious storm in a rotten, sinking smack. He was alone
when the boat was sighted. Whatever had happened to the
rest of the crew, they had not survived and the boy had.
Captain Somerville thought he detected something, a
sharpness in the eye perhaps, or the boy's upright and
defiant stand, that suggested there was a measure of
courage there, or determination, or despair.

'Speak English, boy?'

'Yes, sir.'

'Ever hear of the United Irishmen?

Dónal hesitated.

'No, sir.'

'Liar,' replied Captain Somerville, matter-of-factly.
'Everyone's heard of them. Worst kept secret in the
history of Christendom. Related to one or two of them
myself, as a matter of fact. You weren't expecting to meet
anybody out here on the water, were you?'

Dónal knew that Captain Somerville was questioning
him about the French. Everyone in Ireland knew that the
United Men were daily expecting help from France. There
were frequent rumours of troops landing, but always on

faraway beaches and, in the end, always false rumours.

'I did not, sir.'

'Where's the crew of that boat you were on?'

Dónal did not expect such direct questions. He wondered how best to answer it. He decided to be honest whenever it seemed safe to do so. After all the worst that could happen to him here was that he might be flogged, and he was used to that.

'It was my father's boat, sir. But my father died some time ago. I was living with my uncle and we did not get along, sir. He took to the drink when we fell on hard times. So two nights ago I made up my mind to sail to America.' He looked at the captain to see how he was taking this. 'So I slipped her moorings, sir, and set sail. Out of Cork.' He felt his legs grow weaker.

'Stole the boat, you mean, boy!'

Truth again?

'Yes sir. It used to be my father's boat but we lost her with the bad seasons and the failed harvest.'

'Indeed,' said Captain Somerville, 'times have been hard in Ireland. I heard it. Do you mean to tell me that you fought the smack through the storm on your own? You had no one else aboard?'

'Not a soul, sir.'

The captain looked at him. Gathering courage, Dónal went on, 'I confess I stole it sir. But I had no other means of escaping – of bettering myself.'

Captain Somerville smiled. 'If we were all to better ourselves by stealing, boy, where would the world be?'

'The world would be much the poorer for it, sir,' Dónal replied.

Captain Somerville glared at him for a moment, then burst out laughing. Charlie Madden, standing outside with his ear to the door, smiled quietly to himself.

'By god, sir, you're a son-of-a-gun and no doubt about it. You steal a boat and set sail for America. You ride out that storm in her even though she's as rotten as a tree stump. Then you come into my cabin and make clever remarks.'

'She was not rotten sir! The *Ellen Brice* was a fine boat.'

The captain looked thoughtfully at Dónal. Here was a young lad of spirit, indeed. And his speech was that of a boy with some education. But there was no means by which a boy could make use of his education in the navy and the navy would be this boy's home for this cruise at least. Perhaps, if he stood to his guns and lasted out the voyage he might like it. He might even rise in it. Only gentlemen or rich men became officers, but there were other ranks that a low-born boy might reach – bosun for example, a kind of officer among the men, or even master, if he could study and learn. A master was not quite a captain, yet in big ships he was nearly as important. Masters did all the navigation and the working of the ship in the vessels known as first raters, huge ships like Nelson's *Victory*, with a crew of five hundred men. Captain Somerville looked towards a compass that was swung from the ceiling above his head, as if out of habit, then back at Dónal, and it seemed to Dónal that the captain's face looked almost kindly.

'Well, well, every man loves his first command, what? And this smack, *Ellen Brice* you called her, she was yours. We shall have to find something useful for you to do here.

But I must tell you, my man Best was on board your boat, and I trust every word he says, mind. He tells me you'd have gone down with her in no more than a few hours. No hope for her. Planks rotting, you see.'

'Don't take it hard,' he said, when he saw tears begin to well up in Dónal's eyes. 'She kept swimming until we came along, what? Saved your life, even though she lost her own. That's what I call a good ship. Now run along. You'll be a powder monkey. Feed the powder to the guns. Best or Madden will show you the run of it. There's a good chap.'

Dónal did not leave.

'Go on, I say.'

'Do I have no choice, sir?'

'You'll serve the king, my man. Many a lad of your age and mettle would die for the chance! You'll grow up to be a sailor, swinging from the topgallant in a gale, a jack tar like the rest of them. And with your spirit and a tongue like that I have no doubt you'll be a bosun some day. What more could you want?'

'I would rather be put ashore, sir.'

'What and go back to your uncle? Surely not. Besides, every port in Ireland and England is being scoured for men at this very moment. No sooner would I put you ashore than you'd be picked up by the king's press. They'd knock you on the head and you'd be back aboard before dark. That's their job – to get sailors for the navy. Not to mention, sir, that this ship has her orders, and her orders are to catch those damned French that my country-men at home in West Cork put so much store by, and to sink them, sir. Sink them. Gunner Best will make a powder monkey of you and you shall help us to do our duty. Good day to you!'

He stood up and turned his back on Dónal to look out through the large window set into the stern. Dónal glanced in that direction too, before he left, and with a pang of loss he realised that the *Ellen Brice* was gone, the sea behind them completely empty. Gone down with her were all his hopes and dreams. The food that he had taken with such an uneasy conscience was wasted now, making his crime so much worse. Even the few things that he had gathered from the sea had been taken back by the sea again. All that he had left of property was a one-sleeved jacket and his father's knife. More than all the world he wished himself back on the deck of the *Ellen Brice* again. If he could once return, he told himself, no one would ever prise his hands off her tiller.

4

THE TOPGALLANT

It was Charlie Madden and his friend Gunner Best who
told Dónal the story of how they had found him.

'We was licking our wounds on the *Leander* that day,'
Charlie said. 'That was a mighty storm you stuck out, lad.
We carried reefed courses, which is what we call the
lowest line of sails, and the sail maker is below at this
moment stitching one of 'em. Anyway, along about the
second dogwatch, that'd be in the afternoon to you, the
sea being down a lot and the wind light, the lookout in
the foretop sings out 'Boat ho!', which means he seen you.
The first officer, Mr Wilson, come up to the foretop with
his spyglass and 'A smack' says he, as if we didn't know.
When he come down again the captain and himself put
their heads together and their chins were wagging for five
minutes or more. Best heard what they said, didn't you
Best?'

'I did. They was thinking this was one of your rebel
boats come out to lead a French man-o'-war in. Only from
the cut of your jib they guessed you'd been knocked
about. 'Maybe,' says the first officer, 'they give her the

go-by in the storm. The Frenchman might still be hanging about.'

A gleam came into their eyes whenever they mentioned the French boat, Dónal noticed. They had already explained the prize system to him, how when an enemy boat was captured a small group of sailors and men, called the prize crew, was put aboard her, whose job it was to sail her to some port where she could be sold to the highest bidder. Plymouth was the place they all favoured, being the nearest and busiest. None of them would have a boat sold in Ireland because the price was too low. Once she was sold in Plymouth, the money was divided up into eight parts. Some of it went to the commander-in-chief of the navy, a fact all the men resented. ('What did *that* old billy have to do with a fight, tell us that lad?') The captain got three eighths and could become a rich man if it were a valuable ship. The other officers got their share and finally the crew got two eighths – to be divided equally between them. A battle won was money in the sailors' pockets, which explained why every man on the ship was eager to fight. In the days of the Spanish War, two small frigates had captured a Spanish treasure ship out of South America and the captains had made a huge fortune. Because the crew of these frigates was so small, every man aboard had been made rich by the capture. This, they explained, was a kind of sailor's heaven.

Charlie continued with his story. 'A certain man shouted to the captain from the gun deck, "Sink her, your lordship, it's a trick of the Frenchies!" But our captain is a decent, stout-hearted little man. He told Best and me to lower away the jollyboat and go over to see if she had anyone alive in her at all. Well we pulled lively on our oars, I tell you, because we were still afraid that it was a trap. But as we got closer we could see plain enough that she had had a hard time of it and was sinking fast.'

Best told how they had pulled alongside and climbed aboard, which was not difficult because of how low the *Ellen Brice* was in the water.

''She's rotten through and through,' says I to Charlie Madden. 'Mayhap she'll sink under us.' But we set about it quick like. Picture our surprise when we come on you asleep in the sternsheets. A youngster, on his own in a sinking boat. That were a surprise to us.'

It was Charlie Madden who lifted him, powerful, soft-hearted Charlie, and carried him back to the jollyboat, so it was Charlie's voice that Dónal had heard in his dream.

The Captain and Lieutenant Wilson were waiting to see what was coming aboard.

'''What have you there, Madden," says Wilson. "A child," says I. "That was asleep in the sternsheets. Not a soul else aboard, sir." Well they gaped at the child, I tell you, Dónal a stór. They must have thought you were a cannibal that ate the rest of the crew. Such things do happen, I know. Well they sent me down to the loblolly boy, that's the surgeon's mate, to get you seen to. But when he seen you he says, "Rest is all that boy needs." So we lay you down in the straw beside my gun, as you well remember, and covered you up with a blanket. You come round again at about the start of the first night watch, just before sundown, that being my watch below as it happened, and I was there to see you wake up, my lad.'

Charlie Madden's faced glowed with pleasure at the thought of how he had made Dónal comfortable and seen him wake up and ready to stand. Ever since Dónal had come on board Charlie and Gunner Best had adopted him. They treated him like a son, teaching him about the ship with a father's patience. And Dónal, whose love of the sea knew no bounds, was a quick learner. 'But what happened to my father's boat?' This was the first question in Dónal's mind. How did the *Ellen Brice* go down? What was her end?

His two friends looked uncomfortable. They were sitting among the boats in the upper gun deck, facing into the light westerly breeze and the evening sun. Charlie Madden was stitching a tear in his jacket, and Best was busily tying a complicated knot to decorate the handle of his sea chest.

'She foundered, mate. She just foundered,' Best told him without looking up from his knotwork. 'Down like a stone.'

Dónal did not believe him.

'It's true, mate. I swear to God. Not a word of a lie. She were rotten from her garboard strake to her gunwale.'

Tears welled up in Dónal's eyes. All these years waiting and watching as the *Ellen Brice* sat on the mud and rose to the tide, and she had been rotten all that time. His dream was rotten at the core, rotten as an old tree stump as the captain had told him.

'Whisht, Dónal,' said Charlie Madden. 'Whisht, boy. She kept you afloat, didn't she?'

'Oh, Charlie, I thought she would carry me to America. She was my father's boat and she was the only thing left of him apart from the knife.' Dónal's knife was still tied to his belt.

Charlie Madden looked at Best and some unspoken word passed between them.

Best spoke quietly. 'I'll tell thee the truth, Dónal. But don't take on about it. She didn't founder at all.'

'And that's the truth,' confirmed Charlie. 'Best here is the sharpest gunner in the boat. Tell him, Besty.'

Dónal looked from one to the other, uncomprehending.

'Orders from the captain, mate. I sank her. She went down like a true ship o' the line. A thirty-two pound ball sent her to the bottom and I was the man that laid the gun. Don't take on now, mate. And don't blame me for the sinkin' of your father's boat.'

Dónal's heart lifted. She went down like a ship of the line. That was a brave end for a brave boat, not just giving up the fight like any poor fishing smack, but sunk by gunfire. Sunk by a fine brave man-of-war. And the gun was laid by the sharpest gunner on the ship. He turned to Best and shook his hand. Then, solemnly, he shook Charlie Madden's.

'I thank you for telling me that,' he said, and jumping down from his seat he strode forward to gaze over the side at the water rushing past. 'Goodbye, father,' he said quietly, as if the rushing water held his father's spirit. The time of dreaming his father's dreams was over. Dónal knew he was embarking on another life that he must begin to learn as soon as possible if he was to make the best of it.

Dónal's official title in the roll-call was 'powder monkey'. His job, Best explained, was important only in a fight. For the rest of the time he must strive to learn everything that could be learned about sailing this huge city of a ship that was over one hundred and twenty feet long and had a crew of almost three hundred men. Every one of those three hundred longed for the day when the lookout would shout 'Sail Ho!' and the order would go out to 'Clear for action!'

When the ship they were all hoping for was sighted, Best explained, Dónal would hear a drum. This drum was sounded for all important events on the ship, but this time it would beat a special message. Through the drum the captain would give the order *'to quarters'* and every man aboard would know exactly where to go. All the decks would be cleared for action, even the wall separating the captain's cabin from the rest of the ship would be knocked flat (it was only held in place by wedges) and gunners would take over the guns that fired through the stern windows of the captain's day cabin. From then on Dónal's work was to keep the guns supplied with the packets of gunpowder that were needed to fire the shot.

Each deck had a room that was called the hanging magazine. In here the gunpowder packets were kept but it was too dangerous to keep a lot of them there because if a shot got in, the room would explode. So most of the gunpowder was kept in the main magazine, down below the waterline, on the lowest deck in the ship. This deck was called the orlop deck, though no one knew what the name meant. Dónal would have to keep the hanging magazines supplied with powder from the main magazine. This involved running down the ladders that led from one deck to the next, down into the magazine and back up carrying cloth bags of powder.

Dónal hated the main magazine. It was a strange room, deep down in the ship, and because it was so low it was always cold. The room itself was lined with a metal fire wall and the only light in there came from windows in the wall. No one could risk taking a lantern inside, so the lanterns were hung outside these windows and shed a cold ghostly light into the magazine.

The men who worked there were equally strange. Once a battle had begun they worked in the constant fear of death. If by chance a shot should penetrate to them, not even the fire wall would protect them because cannon shot was still hot when it reached its target. The explosion would be so big that it would break the ship in pieces. The men who worked in the magazine would have no chance of survival. It was rare for a ship to be hit in this way, and in reality the enemy would far rather capture the ship and share the prize money than see it blown into the sky.

Another fear of the magazine men was that the ship's sides would be broken below the waterline and the main magazine would flood. These men grew to accept a constant threat from fire and water. They rarely smiled and, unlike the rest of the crew, they didn't talk much. They were very superstitious and would not allow certain words to be mentioned at all. For example Dónal was kicked for mentioning the word 'fire'. Neither could he mention rabbits, women, drowning or any of the names of the gun captains. All of these, they told him, brought bad luck to the magazine, and bad luck down there could mean the destruction of the whole ship.

Dónal soon got used to the ways of the ship. He learned the names of the decks, the masts and sails, the numerous ropes that raised and lowered sails or turned the square sails into the wind. He learned the different drumbeats that called the men to their food or brought them to attention for the captain to speak to them. He got used to the constant shouting and occasional kicks that the bosuns gave the men as they drove them to carry out their duties ever more quickly. In fact, he realised that being quick in carrying out orders was not just for the sake of the captain or the officers. A crew that could load and fire a gun in ninety seconds would get off more shots than one that took ten seconds longer and so more shot would strike the enemy. Sailors who could trim the sails quickly and efficiently would help the ship to manoeuvre out of difficulty.

All the tasks on board this ship were carried out to the accompaniment of a song and the leader in the songs was called the shantyman. Dónal learned that a good shantyman was highly prized. His song gave the rhythm for the work. The hard work of hauling the yards, for example, was accompanied by a halyard shanty – a slow regular song. The shantyman would sing the line and all the sailors would sing the chorus. The chorus, with perhaps fifty men singing, was always stirring for Dónal to hear, and he soon picked up the simple tunes and words. It pleased Dónal's friends to see him learning their work songs.

The shantyman aboard the *Leander* was an Irishman with the strange name of Thaddeus Gallahoo. He came from Limerick, he told Dónal, and traced his ancestry back to ancient princes. The sailors liked to mock him about that, and often called him Prince Gallahoo. The shantyman did not mind; he even enjoyed the fun. He had one wooden leg and would beat time to the faster songs by hammering the wooden leg on the deck. He could speak Irish, too, and once made up a song about Mr Wilson, the first officer, which was partly in Irish and partly in English. In the English part he praised Mr Wilson and in the Irish part he explained how the men hated him and told the listeners all Mr Wilson's mistakes. The sailors were mightily pleased with the joke, once they had the Irish parts explained to them, and some of them even tried to pick up the strange Irish words.

In the early days Dónal used to look up at the huge masts and see the men seeming to cling like bats as the masts and yards swept across the sky to the rolling of the boat. It seemed to him that to go up there was foolhardy and dangerous, that he would never overcome his fear and climb even to the lowest yard. But Charlie Madden and Gunner Best led him slowly upwards, first to the huge yard that spread the courses or lowest sails. These yards were as big as trees and Dónal felt quite safe clinging to them. He would have been happy to go no higher and considered himself very brave to have got that far. But in a few days he was desperately clinging to the topsail yard and staring into the laughing faces of Best and Madden. In time that too seemed easy.

On the day he perched on the slender yard of the main topgallant sail, he felt he had reached the pinnacle of achievement. He felt ready to become a sailor now. He looked down at the small shapes moving about the decks below him and imagined he was an old Roman god looking down on his people. He waved down to the foretop lookout, who smiled back at him before turning away again to scan the horizon.

It was not long before Dónal was climbing the rigging and working sail with the best of the crew in calm weather, although Captain Somerville's express orders were that he was not to be allowed aloft in any strong wind. He had a quick mind and was ready to learn and this pleased his teachers, Charlie and Best, who took a deep pride in him.

The sailors enjoyed having a boy on board, especially one with a quick wit and a clever tongue. They enjoyed repeating his remarks, recognising that somehow Dónal was more educated than them. They especially enjoyed telling how Dónal had put Mr Wilson in his place in Latin one night.

Mr Wilson was the only man aboard who resented Dónal's presence. Dónal could not be sure why this was so, but suspected it was because the captain had taken a liking to him and more than once had Dónal to serve at the table in his cabin. Then again, perhaps it was because Dónal was an Irishman, and Irishmen made the lieutenant feel uncomfortable. At any rate he took every opportunity to criticise or humiliate Dónal, pointing out his mistakes in clipped, sarcastic tones, and complaining to the captain and other officers that Dónal lacked discipline and would be flogged if he had his way.

Somehow Mr Wilson had got wind of the fact that Dónal had gone to school. In those days most sailors were illiterate. To have a powder monkey who could read Latin and Greek, even a little, was highly unusual. Mr Wilson now began to show off his own Latin whenever the opportunity arose, and the men were quite amused by this. They encouraged Dónal to catch him out and began to place bets on them as if it were a fight of some kind. Whenever Dónal and Mr Wilson were near each other there would be sailors nearby with their ears stretched, hoping to catch every round of the 'Latin battle'. Every evening they asked him if he had tried it yet.

'Board him with the Latin, mate,' they used to say, and it became a catchcry among them. 'Board him, Dónal, board him,' they used to say when he went on duty for his watch. The one thing the sailors knew when they saw it was a good seaman, and they despised any officer who could not manage the ship or command men. Captain Somerville was a fair officer and a fine seaman but Mr Wilson was a bitter man whose temper was easily aroused. He was always bringing men before the captain on one charge or another and there had been a number of floggings since the ship left Spithead in England. The sailors hated the cat-o'-nine-tails, the whip with which these floggings were carried out, and any officer who was keen to use it was hated too. Mr Wilson seemed to take pleasure in seeing men's backs flogged raw. He often referred to what he called 'the bosun's cat' as if it were an animal that lived on the ship. The men did not forgive him for this.

Dónal had been told to wait on deck in case Mr Wilson had any need of the captain. They were steering east-northeast in a failing wind. Everyone was on edge because earlier on the lookout had seen lights off the starboard bow. The captain had turned in to sleep, leaving word that if the lights were sighted again he was to be wakened.

The wind was dying out completely and the moon had gone down when the lookout spotted the lights again. The *Leander* was drifting lazily on a calm sea. Only the highest sails showed any sign of a breeze. The helmsman was looking at the compass with dismay; the boat refused to steer without wind. Behind him was the stiff form of the marine, whose duty it was to strike the bell to indicate the time. Because of the calm, the bell was muffled and could scarcely be heard on the quarterdeck. The only other people on the deck were Dónal and Lieutenant Wilson.

'Light ho,' the lookout hissed. He didn't need to shout because in that flat calm every sound carried and if they could hear it on the quarterdeck so might the enemy.

'Where away,' answered Lieutenant Wilson. He sprang up on to the rail that surrounded the deck and from there climbed up to the lowest step on the mast. In a moment he was down again, muttering under his breath about 'some damn merchant ship'.

'Boy, go below and inform Captain Somerville that we have sighted lights on the starboard bow, not more than three miles hence. Tell him also that we are becalmed.'

The captain was already awake and was on deck before Dónal got to the cabin door. He and Mr Wilson paced to and fro discussing the situation.

'Can't catch him in this wind, Wilson. Nothing to do, I suppose, but wait. Hardly a Frenchman if he's carrying lights anyway, what. Damn fool way to invade a country, showing lights.'

'Shouldn't be surprised with the French, sir.'

'Your Frenchman is no fool, Wilson. Damn fine sailors, if you ask me.'

'Yes, sir.' Wilson knew he had been told off again. He supposed that Captain Somerville, being Irish, was touchy on the subject of nationality. The Irish, in his experience, were a strange lot.

'Merchant vessel, becalmed, I think. What else can she be, what? Unless it's a trick to draw us down on them.'

'Should we clear for action, sir?'

'Good God, no! The men will be all the better for a good night's sleep. When we come up with them in the morning we'll see what happens. We'll know by then what colours she wears.'

'Yes, sir.'

They paced for a few minutes longer. With the moon down, the water lay like black glass all round the ship.

'Keep the boy with you, Wilson. Send him down to me if there's anything to report. Carry on.' And the captain was gone.

'Well, boy,' said Mr Wilson with a bitter edge to his voice, 'you will have no sleep tonight. I should think your Irish bones will give out on you before this cruise is done.' He laughed as if he had said a remarkably clever thing. Dónal sensed, though he did not know why, that the captain's words had wounded Mr Wilson. He felt that Mr Wilson was in turn hoping to hurt him.

'Indeed, sir, I would be letting the captain down if I slept on my duty.'

Wilson was taken aback by that. 'Mind your tongue, boy. I don't take kindly to insolence.'

'I did not think it insolent, sir. I merely answered that I would do my duty.'

This did not please Lieutenant Wilson. His hand was visibly shaking and he seemed to be making a great effort to control himself. 'Your devotion to Captain Somerville is praiseworthy, boy,' he said, as coldly as his anger would allow. 'But I think you lack something in respect for me. I shall bring you before the captain on a charge of insubordination. The bosun's cat will teach you to obey all your superiors.'

It was this last word 'superiors' that started the fire in Dónal's heart. How could he, the son of a United Irishman, who had mastered his own boat and ridden out a storm that others would have died in – how could he tolerate such insult? He remembered the sailors' bet and dredged his mind for something in Latin that might put Mr Wilson in his place. His old schoolmaster came to mind. When he was about to administer the stick he would inform the victim in Latin that what is food to one man is bitter poison to another. The words seemed to fit Mr Wilson very well. Dónal's respect for the captain was bitter poison to the Lieutenant.

'*Ut quod ali cibus est aliis fuat acre venenum*, sir, as Lucretius said.'

A smile creased the helmsman's face, although he never took his eyes off the swinging compass. The rigid body of the marine seemed to relax a little and then straighten up again.

Dónal knew two things as soon as the sentence was out: firstly that Mr Wilson did not understand the words and secondly that by making a fool of him in the presence of the helmsman and the marine he had made an enemy for life. Lieutenant Wilson raised his hand and struck Dónal full in the face. The blow sent Dónal flying across the deck. He lay where he had fallen, trying to staunch the blood which had started to flow from his nose, and looked up to see the officer advancing on him again. There was murder in his eyes. Dónal looked first to the helmsman and then to the marine for help, but neither of them moved or even looked at him. The helmsman's eyes were now fixed on the higher sails. The marine's eyes, as always, were fixed on the horizon directly in front of him. Dónal looked up and saw Mr Wilson lifting his boot to bring it down on him, and then he heard the helmsman say, 'A wind sir. A wind.'

The words halted the kick in mid-air. Mr Wilson hissed at Dónal to fetch the captain and as the boy struggled to his feet he heard him calling for the bosun to rouse the watch. He stumbled down the ladder to the captain's cabin, dimly aware that the ship was moving again.

5
—

MURDER!

Daylight was spreading from the east when the *Leander* fired her signal gun. They could see the captain of the merchant ship consulting with his mate.

Captain Somerville ordered signal flags raised: *Heave to or I will fire on you.* This caused considerable stir on the quarterdeck of the other boat. As the light improved, they could see the name *Provident, Boston* in large letters across her stern.

'An American, by God,' said Captain Somerville. 'No wonder they're edgy.'

The American was obviously weighing up his chances. The breeze was light and if he set all sail it was just possible that the *Provident* would outrun the heavier *Leander*. But if, by any chance, some of the *Leander's* shot fell among his precious merchandise, there would be a considerable loss of profit. In the end he decided to do as he was told.

The men of *Leander* saw the American ship backing her foresail with some satisfaction. It was only proper, they felt, that a humble merchant ship should obey the signals of a man-of-war.

Slowly the *Provident* came to a halt in the gentle breeze. And slowly the *Leander* came up to her, stopping broadside on but a few hundred yards away. Soon a boat was seen to be lowered from the *Provident,* and as it made its way across the gap between the two ships they could see her captain in it.

He came aboard with a sprightly confident air and made straight for Captain Somerville. 'What do you mean by this, sir, stopping my ship like some common pirate?'

Captain Somerville almost smiled at the direct attack. 'Will you take coffee, captain? It's an uncommonly early hour.'

The American refused.

'Very well, then. I must inform you that my crew will search your vessel ... '

'By God, sir, I am no common smuggler. By what right do you search my ship?'

Captain Somerville gestured towards the rows of guns on the upper gun deck, all run out and neatly laid, each gun captain standing ready with the firing lanyard in his hand. 'You can see that this is a ship of His Majesty's navy. You are in our waters, sir.'

'Aye, going about my lawful business.'

'These are troubled times, captain. You may not have heard, but rebellion is afoot in Ireland. The French are daily expected. We must take precautions.'

'Very well then,' the American said. 'I must submit to superior force. You may search my vessel, but I must tell you I resent it.'

'Mr Wilson will take a boat across. Come below sir, and

take coffee and bread with me. It's all I have to offer at this hour of the morning. We've been keeping the sea now for almost two months and my dining room is not well provided.'

The American laughed. 'I made a fast passage from Boston but my coffee ran out three weeks ago. I'd much appreciate a cup.' They went down to the captain's cabin, laughing together, and soon Dónal was summoned to tell his tale to the American captain.

His story had become famous all over the ship. Sailors at sea quickly run out of news. In a month they know every story and in two months they are bored with them, so anything new is like gold to them. Dónal's story was particularly highly thought of because it seemed to them to be almost a fairytale.

In the evenings, when the endless daytime work was over and the sea was calm, whatever watch was off duty could relax at their mess tables. These tables were set up below decks, one table beside each gun. That gun's crew took their food at that table and at night when sleep came on them they slung hammocks above the guns and slept in them.

Sometimes they would call on someone to sing or play a fiddle. Sometimes they would play games with ingenious pieces of timber. Sometimes they would just talk, and when they talked they loved to hear Dónal's story.

'Tell us about your wicked old uncle, Dónal,' they would say. Or: 'Tell us how you sailed that rotten tub.' They were particularly interested in the more lurid parts – like when Dónal's father died of fever or how his uncle used to beat him. Then they would pity him and tell him that he was lucky to be picked up by the *Leander*, because they all seemed to believe that life on a man-of-war was far better than being ashore. Another thing that caught their interest was the detail of how he sailed the smack, how he reefed, the way the squall came on, how he was saved by his lifelines from going over the side, how he could not open his fingers because the muscles wouldn't work. They were forever urging Thaddeus Gallahoo to compose a song about Dónal and his father's rotten smack.

But most of all they loved to hear the story of how he had tricked his uncle and had his revenge for all the cruel treatment. They would begin to chuckle as he told how he mixed the water, oatmeal and salt. The picture of his uncle galloping across the fields with no boots on in search of water made them howl with laughter. Over and over again they would hear this story and eventually Dónal's porridge became a byword with them for anything that tasted bad. They would tell the cook that his watery stew was as bad as Dónal's porridge. Or if Mr Wilson looked put out over something, they would say he looked as if he had tasted Dónal's porridge. 'Aye,' they would say, 'Dónal's porridge is a cruel revenge all right!'

The story became so famous that the captain, over-hearing the men using the phrase, had asked him where it came from. Charlie Madden, standing nearby, piped in that Dónal's adventures were 'like a ballad or an old-time story', and then Captain Somerville had to hear them. Dónal entertained the quarterdeck with it and afterwards, from time to time, the Captain would want to hear it again. That was how Dónal was summoned to the day cabin to tell his story to the American captain.

When he had told it, the American declared it was the best story he had ever heard, if even half of it was true, and the captain assured him that the last part was certainly true and that he could vouch for it. The American was quiet for a while, swilling his coffee in his cup. He was a tall man with broad shoulders and huge hands. Beside him Captain Somerville looked like a bird.

'You say you dreamed of going to America, boy? Now that's a fine thing.'

'I did, sir.'

'Now what would you say, Captain Somerville, if I was to offer this fine boy the chance to get to America? I'd give him a place on my brig. He'd be a cabin boy and in due course when my trading on this side was done I'd take him back to Boston with me. I give you my word that I'd discharge him at the pier head, if that's what he wanted.'

Captain Somerville was silent. 'It's a chance, Captain, you know that. What will happen to the boy on a man-of-war? I guess he'll lose a leg or a hand or an eye in some action with the French, and then what? Or maybe he'll rise to the noble rank of bosun. A boy like this deserves better. He's a cut above the common sailor sure enough. He has a bit of learning. I'd teach him a bit more. A little of this and that. Navigation. He could better himself. What do you say, Captain Somerville?'

Captain Somerville looked directly at Dónal. 'All of what Captain Pearson says is true. I will not stand in your way.'

Dónal hesitated. Here was his chance to get to the New

World, to learn navigation, to be a free man. Yet when all was said and done, was there much difference between a powder monkey and a cabin boy? And what of his new friends? Captain Somerville and Charlie Madden and Best had been kind to him and he had other friends among the crew. American boats had a reputation for cruelty and who was to say that the American sailors would be as kind as the English?

'I thank you, Captain Pearson, but I cannot leave the ship.'

Captain Pearson accepted his reply with a shrug of his shoulders. He finished the dregs of his coffee and he and Captain Somerville stood up. Just then they heard the calls of the bosun as the boat came alongside and presently Mr Wilson was in the room.

'Well, Mr Wilson?'

'All clear, sir. Cargo of New England rum.'

'Very good, Mr Wilson, carry on. Captain Pearson, I wish you a safe voyage. As soon as you clear our ship we will make sail. Good day to you, sir.' The men shook hands and Wilson led the American out.

'That was well said of you, boy,' said Captain Somerville. 'There's more mettle in you than meets the eye. That American met a French ship a few days out. We shall surely come up with her. Then we shall see how you do, what? At any rate, I shall not forget your loyalty. '

As the little brig fell away behind them, Dónal wondered whether he had made the right choice. At any moment they might be plunged into a bloody battle with the French ship, whereas he could just as easily be going peacefully about his business as cabin boy on the American boat, with the prospect of being paid off in Boston and fulfilling his dreams.

Then for the first time he realised that his dreams no longer involved America. The prospect of a fight with the enemy and the prize money that would follow seemed a much stronger attraction. He would make his money in the blood and death of sea battle, then he would buy his own boat.

The bosun was shouting, 'Rouse out there the watch below! Rouse out to shorten sail!' As he shouted, he strode along the line of hammocks and tipped out anyone who was slow off the mark. Dónal, who was already out and pulling on his jacket, got cuffed around the ear. 'All hands to shorten sail! Look lively there! Show a leg!'

Dónal could hear the storm outside, like a rumbling in his head, the dreadful sound of waves crashing against the fragile sides, and coursing across the hatches. Out on deck, Dónal was reminded of his night in the *Ellen Brice*. The fine weather of the past month had finally broken and the wind had built up during the night. The ship was labouring with too much sail up. Mr Wilson, the officer of the watch, had turned out all hands to reduce sail. Already half the men were aloft, struggling with the furious canvas.

Dónal watched in awe as a gust raged through the rigging and men held on for their lives. Such gusts could shake even hardened sailors from their fragile hold. He had heard stories of men falling from the windward side and crashing on to the deck below. Such a fall meant certain death. Falling from the lee side, where the masts tilted out over the sea, was not much better. The ship was racing along at six or seven knots. In one minute anyone who fell over the side would be invisible in the darkness. No officer would attempt to turn the ship in these conditions. To do so would mean the loss of one or all of the masts, and once the ship was disabled she would be at the mercy of the sea.

At such times Dónal's duty was to stand by, ready to do any work that could be done at deck level. All the sailors agreed that he could not live on the yards in such a wind. As he stood there the rain began to come down and he was glad of the black-tarred hat that Gunner Best had given him to keep the rain off his neck. But this was not like the night on the *Ellen Brice* when it seemed as if the sea were going to swallow him. A ship like the *Leander* could weather much worse than this. Mr Wilson had not even ordered storm canvas to be sent aloft. He was simply furling the higher sails and reefing the topsail. Dónal turned to look at the quarterdeck and saw Mr Wilson standing there, apparently unconcerned.

Why had he called all hands for a job that could have been done by the watch on deck? Dónal concluded it was another example of the vicious streak the sailors saw in Wilson. It would not do him to leave the off-duty men asleep in their hammocks below. He must turn them out into the cold and rain for no good reason, and send them down wet and cold to shiver in their hammocks until their turn came to go on duty.

'Send that boy aloft, bosun. No mollycoddling in the king's navy.'

The bosun tipped his cap to Mr Wilson and came down

the deck towards Dónal.

'You're for it my lad,' he told him. 'You'd better go up. Go up to the mainyard, no higher.'

With a sinking feeling Dónal put his foot on the lower ratlines, the rope ladders that ran up the rigging. He did not dare look up or down, but began to climb as fast as he dared. When he reached the mainyard he put his foot in the rope that he was to stand on, wrapped his hand around the spar and began to edge out. He heard someone shouting from below and looked down to see that Mr Wilson had left his place on the quarterdeck and was standing at the foot of the mast. He cupped his hand around his mouth and shouted, 'Higher! Main-topgallant yard! Go up!'

Dónal had never climbed higher than the main-topgallant yard. It seemed to be hundreds of feet above the deck. Up there it was hard to hold on even on a calm day and looking down made him feel dizzy. He began to climb, slowly and carefully, securing each handhold before moving the other, carefully placing his feet on the ratlines as he went. He heard more shouting but did not dare look down. The pressure of wind on his back was terrible. When the gusts came he was forced up against the ratlines as the ship heaved over, then when the ship heaved back he felt as if he would fly off into the air. After a time that seemed like hours to Dónal, he came to the main-topgallant.

Now fear seized him. To climb into the yard he must move his hands from the ratlines to the timber. Then he must move his feet to the rope. He was dimly aware that the sail itself was already furled, and it crossed his mind to wonder why he had been sent up if there was no work to do there. It came to him then that Mr Wilson meant him to fall and die, either with his brains dashed out on deck, or by the slower torment of drowning in the darkness. This thought made him cling even more tightly to the ratlines. The ship heaved and the wind blew and Dónal held on for his life.

Captain Somerville was lying awake in his cabin listening to the wind and the creaking of his ship when he heard the call for all hands to shorten sail. He knew it was Mr Wilson's order. He lay in the warmth of his bed listening to the drumming of feet on the deck and the calls of the bosun. He pitied his men turned out on a cold night and he pitied them for having to go back to their hammocks cold and wet. Not many of his men had more than one set of clothes so most would be sleeping in their wet tunics and breeches.

He had expected the blow. All yesterday the mares' tails, those wispy clouds that foretold a gale, had been drifting across the sky. By evening the cloud was lowering and dark. Rain had arrived during the dogwatches, before the wind had built up at all, and everyone knew the old saying *When the rain comes before the wind topsail sheets and halyards mind.* A gale was coming.

The fine weather had been too good to last. But of course it was easier for the French to sneak through the blockade in a good blow, hiding in the squalls. Yes, this was the weather for the French. He decided to get up and see how things were progressing on deck. Perhaps his presence might embarrass Mr Wilson into ordering the off-duty watch to go below earlier than he otherwise might. He pulled on his clothes and threw his boat cloak over everything. Checking the compass, as was his habit, he noted with irritation that the helmsman was a full two points off course. 'Short rations for you, my man,' he muttered as he went on deck.

He was amazed to find that Mr Wilson was not in his proper place on the quarterdeck. He looked around for some explanation and his eye fell on the helmsman. 'By God, man! Steer by the compass, I say!' he shouted, striding towards him as he said so. The helmsman, who had not seen him come on deck, was so shocked that for a moment he let the wheel go. The angle of the boat increased and Captain Somerville was aware that she was rounding into the wind. Unless she was righted immediately she might capsize, or lose sails or a mast or both. He leapt forward with surprising speed and agility and thrust the helmsman aside. He leant on the great wheel with all his strength and the boat's swing began to slow. Now the helmsman was at his side, putting his weight into it, and gradually the ship came back on course.

Ashen-faced with rage, Captain Somerville cursed the helmsman. 'You shall be flogged for this, by God. You nearly lost me my ship, damn you!'

The helmsman could only point at the mainmast and say, 'Your worship, the boy. Look!'

Captain Somerville's eyes followed his pointing finger to the mainmast and upwards past the courses and reefed topsails, then up and up to the main-topgallant where a tiny figure clung to the ratlines. Then his eye travelled down again and halfway down he saw Gunner Best and Charlie Madden scrambling upwards. Further down again he saw the slight figure of Mr Wilson shouting at the bosun. Even as he watched, he saw the bosun draw a knife and Wilson step back. 'Put your knife away, man,' he heard himself say, although he knew the bosun was too far away to hear him in the gale. If once the bosun threatened Wilson with that knife, his life was as good as over. Captain Somerville would have witnessed it with his own eyes. Wilson would be sure to prosecute the case. There would be no avoiding the sentence Captain Somerville had never yet had to pass. The bosun would be hanged from the yardarm, as sure as this wind would go away.

The bosun held the knife in his hand as if he did not know how it got there. Then he looked up at Mr Wilson. 'You told me to send the boy aloft.'

Mr Wilson watched the knife carefully. Two thoughts were in his mind. Firstly, the bosun was angry enough to kill him. Secondly, if the bosun could be provoked into threatening him, he, Mr Wilson, would see the other man hanged. The second thought made him lick his lips. 'Put your knife away, bosun. The order was all hands. That meant the brat too.'

The bosun looked at his knife again, then he looked calmly into Wilson's eyes. 'You tried to kill him.'

'I'll see you flogged for that charge!'

'And I'll see you in hell!' He darted the knife at Mr Wilson's arm and a spurt of blood spread over the boat cloak. 'Come on, then, me fine cockerel. I'll fight you like a man. I'm no hirish boy!'

Mr Wilson stepped backwards and tripped over something. He fell on his back and before he could recover two men were holding the bosun by the arms. Now a fierce exultation rushed through him. He stood before the struggling bosun and laughed in his face. 'I'll see you hanged from the yardarm, my hirish boy!'

Captain Somerville saw Charlie Madden reach Dónal at the main-topgallant. He saw him tie a rope around Dónal's waist. He saw Gunner Best make the other end of the rope fast around his own waist. Then he saw Madden swing Dónal onto his broad shoulders. Captain Somerville watched them descend, step by step, until they jumped out of the ratlines and on to the deck. Then, out of habit, he checked the steering compass, cast an eye over the sails, glanced up to weather where the rain was coming from and went below. As he went down the steps he saw a sailor passing and called to him to ask Mr Wilson to report to him in his cabin as soon as possible.

He had got his boat cloak off and was sitting at his desk when Wilson knocked and entered.

'You called for me, sir.' Wilson was nursing his arm in such a way as to draw attention to the blood. Captain Somerville looked at it with distaste.

'Mr Wilson, I want you to know that I witnessed the entire proceedings. It will not reflect well on your record if it should come to a court-martial. We must keep the sea until we are relieved, and at present it would not be possible to bring the bosun to trial. Not while we are in a state of readiness. It would be bad for the men to have to see a court-martial. They would be upset by it.' At this Wilson snorted. Captain Somerville felt his anger rise. 'These are the men who must fight the ship, sir! It is important that they fight the French. I have seen them turn on an officer, sir, and it is not a pretty sight.'

He pointed at Wilson's bloody arm.

'These things happen at sea. We must make the best of them. I will offer you the following satisfaction, sir. I shall break the bosun for the attack. In his place I shall appoint Charlie Madden.' Wilson looked angry. He did not like Madden, and Madden was Irish.

'Yes, Mr Wilson, Charlie Madden is a fine seaman. Next I shall flog the bosun to the extent that the law allows. How say you, Mr Wilson?'

'Sir, I demand that their Lordships of the Admiralty be informed that I do not agree with your sentence. I consider that my honour has not been served.'

'Your honour! This is a ship of the line, man! We are at war! Your honour or mine is not worth a pinch of salt! How came you to call all hands tonight? How came that boy to be in the maintop when I had ordered that he not be sent aloft in foul weather? I put it to you, sir, that you have behaved with unnecessary cruelty. Quit my sight. I will hear no more of this!'

6

THE FRENCH ARE ON THE SEA

The French are on the sea,
They'll be here without delay,
And old Ireland will be free,
Says the Shan Van Vocht.

Dónal fell out of his hammock and rolled out of the way of the running feet. Everywhere there was shouting and running and the noise of bulkheads closing away and gun ports opening, but over it all was the dreadful roll of the drum.

'That's *Beat to Quarters,* Dónal,' Charlie Madden shouted. 'We've seen the French.'

Still sore from his climb to the maintop, Dónal pulled on his breeches and his tarry jacket. All around him men were rolling hammocks and stowing them against the ship's sides to reduce the risk of splinters flying. The gun ports were open and he could see the white rush of waves outside. At every gun, men of the gun crew were straining at the tackles to run the gun out. Others were carrying cannonballs from the shot locker to place them near the guns. The ramrods, the reamer, the sponging stave were all down in their battle places.

'Powder, Dónal, boy,' shouted Gunner Best. 'Powder for the magazines!'

Dónal set off at run along the deck, dodging nimbly among the men and guns. He arrived at the ladder that took him down and stood aside as a man carrying wadding came up. He darted down and along the orlop deck to the magazine. The captain of the magazine was already piling the bags along the rack outside. 'Be quick,' he shouted. He wanted to get his powder out and then go back inside the metal door.

For half an hour Dónal ferried the bags of powder up from the main magazine to the gun decks. By then the ship had settled down to a tense silence; only the sailing orders could be heard over the sound of the water. Dónal joined Gunner Best and Charlie Madden where they stood between their thirty-two pounders.

'What's the news?' he asked breathlessly.

'French man-o'-war to windward. She's coming down on us fast.'

'Is that good?'

Charlie shook his head.

'That's bad because she has the weather gage. She can do what she likes, steer where she likes, while we can only sail on a taut bowline. She can twist and turn like a kicked dog. We're stuck the way we are. 'Course we could turn tail and run down the wind.'

'Would that be better?'

Charlie shook his head again. 'No. That'd be worse, I'm thinking. Firstly because we'd be cowards and then again because she'd chase us into the lee of the land and we'd be trapped.'

'What will the captain do, so?' Dónal asked, his mind confused by all these equally bad possibilities.

Charlie grinned broadly. 'Why, he'll fight like he's always done, Dónal, a stór.' He clapped Dónal on the back. 'Cheer up, lad. If we all do our duty we'll shorten that Frenchie's sail for him!' The other gun crews laughed happily. The laughter was infectious and soon Dónal was happy too. He peered out through the gun port like the rest of them to see if he could catch sight of the enemy sail.

The gale of last night had blown out again and the wind was light, so the battle was a long time in beginning. An eerie silence had descended on the whole ship, and to break it the captain sent word for Thaddeus Gallahoo.

'Gallahoo,' said the captain. 'I love a song above all else. Sing us something to put the fire of battle into us.' All the men smiled at this remark, knowing that neither they nor the captain needed a song to put fire in their bellies now that their enemy was swimming into the guns. But Thaddeus Gallahoo struck up 'Hearts of Oak', the warlike anthem of the royal navy, and by the second line every voice in the ship was singing it. The French were surprised to hear the strains of a song rising from the distant English ship. It merely confirmed their view that ordinary English sailors, and their officers, were mad.

About an hour after they had cleared for action, Captain Somerville ordered pea soup and a tot of rum to be served to all the men. Each gun crew took it in turns to take their rum and eat the watery pea soup. When

Charlie and Dónal got theirs, they took it to the steps leading to the middle deck and sat down. Dónal asked Charlie what the fight would be like, and Charlie became very serious.

'Keep runnin', Dónal,' he said. 'Don't stop at all at all. Keep the powder coming up. Every gun on this ship fires once in one hundred seconds. Think, boy. We have twenty-five thirty-two pound guns down here on the lower gun deck. Twenty twenty-four pounders on the middle deck and I won't mention the lighter guns topsides. That's a terrible lot of powder. If we can shoot more roundshot into them than they can shoot into us, they'll strike their colours and give up. That's all there is to it. More powder and shot. So keep runnin'.'

By leaning out of the gun port and looking along the side of the ship, Dónal could make out the captain leaning on the rail of the quarterdeck with his spyglass to his eye. 'What's he doing, Dónal?' someone asked him.

'He's studying her through his glass.'

'And what's the Frenchman doing?'

'She's holding on her course.' Dónal could see her clearly now, the big bluff bows and the majestic wing-like sails gleaming white against the grey sky. 'She's coming straight down on us.'

'She'll turn soon enough. For the broadside,' someone said.

'She will. Or she'll keep coming and lay us aboard.' The French ship might actually come alongside the *Leander* and try to take her by boarding. For this eventuality every man on board had either a cutlass or a boarding pike – a long handle with a vicious spike on the top. Dónal thought of his own knife and wished he too had been given a fine broad cutlass like everyone else.

'How far away now?'

'Near enough a mile,' someone said. The captain would not begin to fire unless she was closer than a mile. That was the furthest the thirty-two pounders could reach. Even at that range the heavy shot would penetrate an oak wall two feet thick but the captain certainly would wait until she was closer than half a mile.

Time seemed to pass with incredible slowness. Dónal had not drunk his rum because he had made up his mind never to touch spirits. Instead he had given his portion to Charlie Madden. Now his throat was so parched he wished he had it again. He was tempted to drink from the bucket of water that the sponge was wetted in, but he knew it was saltwater and would only make him worse. When would this battle start? Whenever he had heard about sea battles he had always imagined them to be sudden affairs, not this drawn-out agony that he was going through. And the worst of it was that down here on the lower gun deck he had no idea what was happening. He felt blind, as if his whole life was being directed by a remote being called Captain Somerville. How did he ever get into this mess? he asked himself. Wasn't he better off ashore, wicked uncle or no wicked uncle? The devil you know, he thought, is better than the devil you don't know.

Dónal noted a change in the way the ship was sailing, and at the same time he noticed the gun crews, who for the past half hour had been lounging about, taking up their battle stations at the gun. Almost at the same moment a spout of water gushed though an open gun port, and a crashing sound came from the upper deck. Within a few seconds he heard a loud rolling sound and realised that it was the sound of the French broadside.

Why didn't Captain Somerville fire back? He watched the gun crews in frozen amazement. Did they know the French were firing at them?

After a time he heard the rolling sound again, but this time it was not preceded by the crashing or the spouts of water. Then he heard cheering from the upper deck which was picked up by the crews. The ship resounded with cheering and he was sure no one but the upper deck knew what they were cheering for.

Now each of the gun captains turned towards the officer who was standing at the foot of the main ladder. He had his head cocked to one side, listening for orders from above.

To Dónal, everything seemed to be happening in slow motion. He saw the officer consult a pocket watch, still waiting.

There was a tremendous crash from the upper deck, followed by screams and running feet, and almost immediately that rolling thunder of the French guns.

'Steady, my lads,' the officer said. To Dónal he seemed unnaturally calm. Then he saw him stiffen, answering someone on the deck above. 'Right, my lads. Fire as she bears.'

Almost immediately the first gun on the deck crashed and leaped back on its tackle, smoke billowing from its mouth. It was quickly followed by the second, then the third and so on. Dónal saw Best's gun recoil and the crew restraining it. A man shoved the reamer down to take out any fragments of burning wadding. Then another dipped the sponge to clean and cool the inside. The bag of powder was stuffed down and tapped into place with the ramrod. Then a portion of wadding followed, was tapped into place and followed by the ball itself. The gun captain pierced the powder bag through the touchhole, inserted the quill and cocked the flintlock. The gun was run out and Gunner Best sighted along the barrel to 'lay' the target. He stepped back quickly and pulled the lanyard and the gun exploded again, crashing back on its tackle, filling the whole deck with acrid smoke. Then the whole process began again.

Dónal saw that this was happening at every gun and he became aware that the same crashing sounds were coming from the deck above. The fight was on.

'Powder, for God's sake.'

Dónal heard the shout and was running before he knew it.

Broadside after broadside.

The broadside of a man-of-war is a terrible thing to think about. Forty guns all pointed at one ship. A thousand pounds of metal crashing into that ship's sides, tearing at the rigging, breaking the masts and spars. Every shot that struck home would send splinters of wood up to a foot long flying in all directions. One could blind you or kill you. Yards as big as small trees would come tearing down on to the deck, bringing rope and tattered sail with them. Then there was the sailors' nightmare – grapeshot and chainshot. Sometimes the lighter guns on the upper deck fired chainshot – two half balls linked by a length of chain – to break the lines that held the masts up. This chainshot would come whistling along in the smoke and if it struck a man it could take his head off as neatly as if a butcher had done it. Grapeshot was made up of hundreds of small pieces of metal. A broadside of grapeshot could clear a whole deck of men in an instant, and leave nothing but groaning wounded.

It was broadside after broadside all that afternoon.

Dónal saw holes in the ship's sides. He saw men being carried down to the surgeon with arms missing, legs missing, with terrible gaping wounds, blinded or stunned, sometimes obviously dead. He saw a cannon break its breaching tackle and go ripping across the deck, killing two of its crew. He saw a man with a piece of timber sticking from his chest and still alive.

He saw so many terrible sights that he stopped looking in the end. He ran like a blind man from magazine to magazine. Most of the time the smoke, trapped between the floor and the ceiling, was so thick he could scarcely see where he was going. To his right and left he saw men with blackened bodies, streaming with sweat and sometimes blood. He didn't ask how the battle was going. He didn't care any longer. He felt like an animal scuttling along the back of a ditch, running from the dogs. His limbs were sore, sorer than they had ever been before, even after his uncle's beatings. His head ached from the continual roaring of the guns.

Broadside and broadside.

At some point he noticed that there was not so much noise. He wondered whose guns were falling silent – the *Leander*'s or the French?

Later still, Gunner Best was wounded. Dónal saw him carried below but could not stop to ask how he was.

Dónal could hardly think.

Yet it seemed to him that the men were cheering.

Somewhere in the smoke and the gathering darkness he could hear the gun crews cheering. And the guns were silent. Was the battle won? Or was this like the cheering he had heard before they had fired on the French? Something with no purpose? Some pointless naval tradition of cheering?

Charlie Madden grabbed his arm. 'Run down and find out how Besty is,' he told him.

'But Charlie, what way is the battle?'

'The day is ours, lad. Go down to Best. Ask the loblolly boy if Best isn't able to talk.'

The loblolly boy gave Dónal a clout on the ear and told him to get out. Dónal was not sorry to go because the room was full of the groaning of wounded men. There was blood everywhere and even as he stood at the door he saw the surgeon take up a saw that was covered in blood and bits of skin and bone.

'Best is all right,' the loblolly boy told him before he gave him the clout on the ear. 'It was a splinter. We got it out easy enough. If things wasn't going our way so easy we'd 'a' sent 'im back up to 'is gun. Now get out.'

When Dónal got back the crews were already organising the deck. Most of the smoke had drifted out again and battle lanterns were hung from the ceiling. Charlie Madden was waiting for him.

'He's grand, Charlie. The loblolly boy said it was a splinter and they got it out. They'd have sent him back only it was going our way so easy.'

Madden spat on the deck. 'It wasn't so easy as all that. Wait till that surgeon gets up on deck. He'll see a sight that'll strike him dumb!'

Dónal wondered what kind of a sight would greet the doctor that would be worse than the dirty bloody room he was working in now.

'Foremast gone from the forecourse up. Not a sail but has been shot to pieces. All the mainyards come a crashing down on deck. It's a terrible sight, surely. The captain's barge is wrecked,' he added as if this were the ultimate sorrow. 'Purely wrecked, it is. I been topsides, see. I seen it meself, Dónal.'

'Did you see the French boat, Charlie?'

'I did. Only the stump of the mainmast left standing. We'll have to tow her in to Waterford. Sorra the prize money we'll get out of her.'

Dónal was not to know that the moment a prize was taken the sailors began to worry about the damage they had done to her. While she was the enemy she had to be shot to pieces as efficiently as possible, but as soon as she surrendered, the sailors began to wish they could have taken her without doing so much damage. This was natural, since the prize was theirs now and they would get their share of her in due course.

Dónal was on deck to see the French captain rowed across. He came on board carrying his battle flag which he handed to Captain Somerville. He then unbuckled his sword and handed that to him too. Then Captain Somerville and the Frenchman shook hands as though they were old friends. Wine and glasses had been placed nearby on the quarterdeck and the captain poured some and handed glasses to the French captain and the other officers present. Then there was a kind of comedy where all the English officers raised their glasses and drank to 'the King, God Bless him', but the Frenchman did not drink. Next came a toast to the brave French, and again all the English drank. Finally all raised their glasses to 'the War', including the Frenchman.

Dónal wondered about this and was told that it was Captain Somerville's way. He liked to make the captured captain feel at home. All the sailors agreed that the French captain must be very upset at the loss of his ship and they even seemed to feel sympathy for him.

Dónal could not understand. Only an hour before the fight they had been swearing and threatening to sink him and all his crew. Now they were wishing him good health and sympathising with him over the damage *they* had done to his ship.

'Ach,' said Charlie Madden, 'sure he's only a sailor like the rest of us. If it fell out that it was that Frenchman that took us, wouldn't you want him to give our captain a glass of wine to console him?'

Thaddeus Gallahoo was already busy with a new song during that night, as the crew worked to cut away the damaged rigging and spars. By daylight they were beginning to work on what was left of the masts and he had hammered out the words of 'Captain Somerville and the Frenchman' . The sailors all pronounced it good and took up the words, Dónal along with the rest. Even Captain Somerville himself seemed to be pleased with it.

Come all you warlike sailors that on the seas do
wander,
I'll tell you of a fight my boys on the man-of-war
Leander,
'Tis of an Irish captain his name was Somerville,
With courage bold it did unfold he played his part
so well.

'Twas on the eighth of May my boys when at
Spithead we lay
On board there came an order our anchors for to
weigh,
Bound for the coast of Ireland, our orders did run
so,
For us to cruise and not refuse against a daring foe.

We had not sailed many lengths at sea before our
ship we spied,
She being some lofty Frenchman, come a bearing
down so wide,
We hailed her across my boys, they asked from
whence we came,
Our answer was from old Spithead, *Leander* is our
name.

'Oh pray are you some man-of-war,' the Frenchman
then did say,
'Then,' replied our captain, 'it's that you soon shall
see
Come strike your foreign colours or else you shall
heave to,

Since you're so stout you shall give out or else we
will sink you.'

The first broadside we gave to them it made them
for to wonder
Their mainmast and their rigging came a-rattling
down like thunder.
We drove them from their quarters they could no
longer stay,
Our guns did roar we made so sure we showed
them English play.

So now we've took that ship me boys God speed us
fair winds
That we might sail to Plymouth town if the heavens
do prove kind
Drink a health to Captain Somerville and all such
warlike souls,
To him we'll drink and never flinch, another flowing
bowl.

7

The Enemy Landed

To everyone's surprise there were no troops on the French ship. She was a seventy-four-gun frigate *Indomptable*, and from her log book the captain could clearly see that she had been at the same game as the *Leander*. She had cruised first in the western approaches to the English Channel and then along the south coast of Ireland. They must have passed her several times but she was considerably further off the coast than they were so they would not have seen her sails. The gale of the previous night had brought her closer and her lookouts had spied *their* sails. She too was after prize money and that was how they had come to join battle.

So where was the French invasion force? Someone who overheard Mr Wilson and Captain Somerville in conversation reported that the officers had, in truth, been expecting at least six ships of the line and as many as five thousand men. Their orders had been to attack, to harass, to hinder a landing but above all to report the arrival of the French squadron to the watch on shore. Companies of Fencibles, men whose sole purpose was to keep watch for a landing had been posted on all major headlands. They would carry the *Leander*'s signals on horseback to Cork or Waterford, and word would reach one of the English commanders, General Cornwallis or General Lake almost before the French could drop anchor. That was the theory at least.

And the *Leander* had done her part.

But where was the French squadron?

The man who overheard the conversation also reported that *Leander* and *Indomptable* were indeed bound for Waterford, not Plymouth. This caused general disappointment in the men. The ship could not be assessed as a prize in Waterford, nor in Cork for that matter. She would have to be repaired in Waterford then sailed on to Plymouth. That meant putting off the question of prize money perhaps another month. The only consolation was that Mr Wilson seemed to have forgotten the fight with the bosun, perhaps believing that his part in it had not been an honourable one. At any rate, the bosun had not been flogged, though he was no longer bosun, and everyone hoped that their success in the fight had put all that out of Mr Wilson's head.

They now crowded sail on what was left of the masts. The foremast was virtually useless and the carpenters, sail-makers and riggers had spent all day inventing an arrangement that would put some useful sail on what was left of it. The captain feared that the mainmast too had been badly weakened and would not allow anything above the topsail. Since this caused the ship to be unbalanced, they had to shorten sail on the mizzen also. The *Indomptable* was in much worse condition and could barely make two knots through the water even though they had her in tow. So it was a slow procession that made its way towards the Irish coast.

Their slow approach allowed them time to take in any unusual sights along the coast. From a great way off smoke was visible and the sailors, who had little to do with so little sail set, crowded the decks and speculated endlessly on what the smoke meant. But as the coast became more clearly visible they could see many fires burning in villages along the shore and on hillsides further back. In places they could see the charred ruins of farmhouses and fields blackened by burning.

A tense silence fell over the crew.

The *Leander* and *Indomptable* slowly inched towards the shore over a summer sea, and it seemed to Dónal that the destruction of the battle had spread itself to the whole world. Wherever he looked on board he saw the wounded lying on deck in the sun, the holes in the bulwarks that the carpenters were patching, the smoke-blackened gun ports. Wherever he looked on shore he saw the same signs of suffering and violence. Only the sea seemed untouched by man's cruelty. The waves sparkled in the August sunshine, throwing strange lights on the ceilings between decks and relieving the dullness in the eyes of the wounded.

He saw the Saltee Islands with their million birds pass close on the starboard side. Then Hook Head was on the starboard bow and the great strand of Tramore swept out beyond Brownstown. The ships were carried by the tide and a light following breeze into the arms of Waterford Harbour. They dropped anchor above Duncannon to wait for a pilot to guide them up the river.

There was an eerie stillness in the harbour. The shore on either side was high and sheltered them from all but the lightest breeze. As darkness fell a great harvest moon rose over the Wexford shore, but there were no lights in the houses and villages that lay all around them.

At dawn they saw the pilot boat put out from Ballyhack and come quickly downriver. An important looking soldier sat on the thwart seat, wrapped in a cloak against the morning air. He came aboard unsteadily and was met by Mr Wilson, who quickly led him to the quarterdeck. His first words were 'The French have landed, sir!' Captain Somerville's face went ashy white.

'Where, sir?'

The soldier pulled a packet from inside his cloak. 'Dispatches, sir. From General Cornwallis to His Majesty's forces at sea and on land.'

Mr Wilson and Captain Somerville scanned the first dispatch and Dónal stood on tiptoe behind the captain to look over his shoulder. Later Charlie Madden questioned him 'What did it say, Dónal? In plain English?'

Dublin Castle, August 1798
It appears by Advices received from the Honourable Major General Hutchinson, dated Castlebar, 26th in the Evening, that the Enemy under General Humbert had landed and secured Killalla but had not attempted to move out. Their three Frigates had sailed from the Coast. The Major General expected shortly to be in force to move against the Enemy. The Province of Connaught continues in perfect Tranquillity.

'Killalla? That's on the *west* coast, by God! Then this fellow in the *Indomptable* was a trick, what. To draw us down here so those three frigates could evade our blockade!'

'I pray you turn over, sir. There are further advices only two days old.' The old soldier seemed to be as excited as Dónal. He hopped from foot to foot, watching the faces of the captain and first officer. Every now and then he gave a little cry of impatience.

Captain Somerville took the second sheet out of the packet.

Dublin Castle, August 1798
Advices were received last Night from Lieutenant General Lake, by which it appears, that early on the Morning of the 27th the French attacked him in his Position near Castlebar, before his Force was assembled, and compelled him, after a short Action, to retire to Holymount. The Lieutenant General regrets that six Field Pieces fell into the Enemy's Hands; but states that the Loss of the King's Troops, in Men, has not been great.

Captain Somerville looked up. 'That idiot General Lake lost six field guns and had to *retire* before a small force of Frenchmen? Do you think, sir, that we, in the *Leander*, would have retired had the *Indomptable* got the better of us? By God, sir, we would have stood to our guns while the ship remained to fight with. The loss of the King's troops has not been great! Indeed!'

'I pray you consider, Captain, that our best intelligence puts the French force at one thousand men and innumerable of the Irishry have risen and swelled his forces. Consider also, Captain, I pray, that General Humbert is a general of considerable experience and his troops are veterans, sir. Veterans.'

Captain Somerville glared at him. 'Do not talk rubbish on my quarterdeck, sir. I am not accustomed to it. What of the rebellion in the County of Wexford?'

The soldier straightened his back and smiled. 'Quenched, Captain. Not a rebel remains in the field; the remnants have gone to ground, cowards that they are. The most notorious of them have already been hanged. Across the river, Captain, you may just see Geneva Barracks where the hangings go forward apace. It has been a satisfactory campaign, Captain.'

Captain Somerville turned away. 'A satisfactory campaign? Captain, you and your General Cornwallis were held at bay for months by a few thousand farmers, paupers, priests and one or two gentlemen – some of whom are acquaintances of mine, by the way. These cowards, as you call them, would have done justice to the name of soldier, when your militiamen and yeomen were better called cowards, running away when the peasants stood up to them with pikes.'

'I am a regular myself,' the soldier replied angrily, 'but I feel obliged to defend the honour of the militia and the yeomanry who have so . . . '

'Very well, sir. Defend the pitchcappings and floggings, the burnings and persecution that drove poor people to fight for their lives. Be so good as to defend that, sir.'

The soldier turned on his heel and was about to leave when Captain Somerville called him back. 'Are you forgetting? You came aboard, I assume, to bring me my orders?'

The soldier made an effort to control himself. 'You are to remain at anchor here. Do not allow your men to come ashore on any account. When it is considered safe, you will be brought up to Waterford where your battle-damage will be made good. Good day, Captain. I will convey your displeasure to Dublin Castle.'

'Do so,' replied Captain Somerville, nothing daunted. 'And convey my opinion that the prosecution of this campaign has been as incompetent as it has been ill-informed.'

Mr Wilson smiled. Perhaps, being on the wrong side of Captain Somerville might not be so dangerous after all. If remarks like that were conveyed to the Admiralty, who knows what would come of them?

'Mr Wilson, inform the men that there will be no shore leave. Strike down the topmasts, and instruct the carpenters to continue with what repairs they can until such a time as fresh timber can be got aboard. Oh, Mr Wilson, lay out the second bower anchor. I suspect we may be a considerable time here. Convey that instruction also to the prize crew aboard the *Indomptable*. We do not want our prize to drag her anchor and blow ashore in a gale.'

As darkness fell on their second night at anchor, Dónal and Charlie Madden sat by their gun. Like everyone else they were wondering what was happening ashore. In ordinary times, Gunner Best would have been with them. His wound was slight and once the splinter had been drawn he was on his feet again. But tonight Charlie and Dónal felt different. This was Ireland, their home, not

Best's. As good as Best was, and they could not ask for a better friend, he did not understand what was in their hearts.

'We should go ashore, Charlie. Have a look. See what's been happening. I wonder if the trouble spread to Cork?'

'We can't. You heard the captain. All shore leave cancelled.'

'We could swim.'

'Not me, lad. I swim like a stone. Never bothered to learn. If you fall out of a ship out there, you might as well drown quick as slow. Swimming is the slow way.' He smiled weakly. 'Besides, the current would beat you.'

'What about the jolly boat?' The jolly boat was lying on a long rope from the stern. Mr Wilson had been using it to go over and back to the *Indomptable*.

'Desertion, Dónal. If we go ashore now we'll be for the high road. Two Irish sailors leaving their ship. This is not a good time.'

'But could we do it? Could we take the boat?'

Charlie smiled. 'Sailors have been going ashore for centuries without their officers knowing. 'Course we could. But if they get caught it's a flogging. Fair enough. Sometimes, after a long voyage it's worth a flogging to get ashore. See the ladies. Drink your ale. But, lad, you know as well as I do what's happening ashore. It won't be a flogging for us. Especially if that Wilson has his way. You know he hates you. And me too, surely.'

Dónal thought for a moment. 'Suppose we had Gunner Best with us. He's English. Then they couldn't accuse us of deserting the ship. It'd be just a flogging if we were caught.'

'Besty would do it for us. But we'd be dragging him into our trouble.'

'I have to find out, Charlie.'

Mr Wilson was bored.

How long would they be left at anchor here? There were over two hundred French prisoners to be fed and rations had been reduced. The men were uneasy. There was no prospect of going up to Waterford for days, possibly even weeks. Even to go up would be poor comfort, since he had hoped that they would put into Cork and he could impress Miss Halpin with his story of the battle and his share of the prize money. Since the incident with the bosun and that infernal Irish boy, Captain Somerville had hardly spoken to him except to issue orders.

Mr Wilson considered that he had behaved with distinction in the fight with the *Indomptable* and expected some word of praise from his captain but Captain Somerville seemed to treat his actions as no more than could be expected. He was continually praising his men and had even mentioned one or two of the junior officers, but Mr Wilson was never mentioned. Wilson knew very well that if he were ever to secure a command for himself he would have to be recommended by his captain. *This* captain, it seemed, could barely stand him. His thoughts turned to scheming for another ship as soon as they put into port. Perhaps if he wrote to his family they might use their influence to have him transferred to some first-rate ship of the line, preferably in the China station, or the West Indies, but as far away as possible from that ignorant

Captain Somerville and his accursed Irish shore.

As he took his turn on the quarterdeck, hoping that the pacing to and fro would restore the warmth to his legs, he thought he heard a sound in the water. Could it be a party of Irish rebels attempting to seize the ship? But the soldier had said the insurrection had been put down here and the leaders hanged. What then? Someone leaving the ship?

He peered over the side. The moon was high and the water calm. There was nothing on the larboard side. He rushed to starboard. Nothing there. He sent the marine, on duty by the bell, to go forward to the bow and look there, while he himself stared at the water astern. Did he detect a movement? Something was missing?

The jolly boat. Listening carefully he could detect a slight slipslop of water. Oars. On an impulse he went below, ignoring the marine's 'all clear', and strode along between the hammocks of sleeping men to Madden's gun. Madden's hammock was full of wadding shaped to look like a human form, as was the boy's.

Now, thought Mr Wilson. Now I have them. They will hang for desertion.

He returned to his post on the quarterdeck. In the morning their absence would be discovered and a party of marines would be sent to recover them. Mr Wilson had no doubt, since the country was alive with redcoats and militiamen, that Madden and the boy would be taken in less than a day. He would await their return with the greatest satisfaction.

8

ENCOUNTER WITH A SPY

The shadow of a stone pier was ahead of them. Quietly dipping their oars, they pulled towards it. They hauled the boat up on to the strand and tied the rope to an iron ring. The tide was falling and the moon was low in the western sky. On their return there would be no moon. So much the better.

They made their way through the silent village. Here and there the thatched roof of a house had been burned out or the doors and windows were broken in. At the end of the village they came upon a milestone. Waterford 1 mile.

They set off as fast as their unsteady legs could carry them. Before long they found themselves wandering through the outskirts of the town. Twice they almost walked straight into a watch. The first time it was a man on his own, quietly smoking his pipe with a large cudgel over his shoulder, but on the second occasion it was a company of militiamen, tramping down a dark backstreet, muskets on their shoulders. They pressed themselves into the shadows of a gateway and moved on more carefully when the watch had passed.

With a sailor's unerring instinct for the water, they found themselves on the quay. Here the usual squalid taverns and inns lined the waterfront; they could be sure of finding some open at any hour. They noticed, as they moved along looking for the right place, that the merchant shipping moored along the quay was all guarded. Eventually they found a light in a doorway and a glance through the window showed them candlelight and a glowing fire.

There were none of the usual clients of the dockside taverns – the naval men, the sailors, the crimps who hired sailors for the boats, the women who always followed sailors.

Dónal and Charlie and Best sat at one side of the room and across the room at a table sat four silent men. The landlord served Charlie and Best two flowing tankards of ale and a glass of milk for Dónal.

'Now, lads,' he said. He smiled benignly on them, a great fat face supported by rolls of flesh. 'Drink up lads. There's more in the barrel.'

Charlie and Best tilted their tankards, drank deep and smacked their lips as they put the tankards back.

'Many's the long day I waited for that glass of beer, landlord,' said Charlie. 'Even the poor lad here didn't taste milk this past two months or more!' He and Best laughed uproariously at this joke. The landlord's fat face opened up in a smile.

'Tell us,' began Charlie, 'how is poor old Ireland, at all? We're away so long we hardly know the place.' Throughout all the exchange Best had remained silent except to smack his lips, his eyes bent carefully on his tankard.

The landlord leant on the counter and lowered his voice. 'The way it is, lads, there's no trade at all. The war is over and the harvest ruined, sure enough, but them yeomen are out the streets every night. Sure you'd be afraid of your life to step out for a drop in a decent man's tavern like this. It's not long since that we had a curfew and no one could go out at all.'

'Where was the fighting?'

'East to Wexford and up to Wicklow. 'Tis all over now.'

'What about the French? Did they come?'

'They did not, bad luck to them. They let us down, there's no doubt about it.'

One of the men at the other table stood up. He seemed hesitant, then straightened his shoulder and strode up to them.

'You're asking a lot of questions, sailor.'

Charlie stood up. 'I have a right. As much right as anyone to know what happens in my own country.'

The stranger looked at his clothes. 'You're a sailor all right. And by the cut of you, I'd say you're navy men. I'd say your country is a hundred miles away across the water.'

Charlie made to reach out for the stranger's arm, but before he could do so the man stepped back and Dónal saw with horror that there was a pistol in his hand. He must have taken it from inside his coat.

'You stand in peril of your life, sailor, believe me. Now answer my questions.' Best had risen at the sight of the gun. 'You sit down. Tell me this; what ship are you off?'

Charlie hesitated.

'It is not one of the merchant ships. None of their men has stepped ashore after dark for weeks. There is an English ship anchored above Duncannon and she has a captured French frigate with her. Is that where you come from?'

'You know what you're talking about.'

'You are Irish. From Cork, by your accent.'

'Cove.'

'What about him and the boy?'

'The boy is from Cork like myself.'

'And the other? We mean him no harm.'

'English.'

'Name?'

'My name is Madden. That's Best and the boy is Dónal Long.' At the mention of Dónal's name one of the other men came over.

'What's your name again, boy? And where do you hail from?'

'Dónal Long, sir, from the County Cork. Ballymonas.' The strangers exchanged glances, then the second man went back to his table.

'Mr Best,' said the man with the gun, 'I'd trouble you to step over and have a drink with my friends. They are quite hospitable. I'd like a word with my countrymen here.'

He sat down with Dónal and Charlie, returning the pistol to the folds of his coat, and for a time he questioned them about the ship. They told him no more than what any dockworker would know – how many guns she had, what was her complement of men, who the officers were. He could have found this out anywhere in Waterford, but he seemed satisfied. They asked him about the rebellion and he told them how the Wexford people had risen, how they had taken Camolin, Enniscorthy, Wexford Town itself, how they had eventually suffered a huge defeat at Vinegar Hill. Most of the leaders were taken and many had already been hanged. Hundreds of prisoners were awaiting execution or transportation in every town in Munster, he said. He gestured towards the window. 'If it was daylight now you'd see their prison ship just down the river in the anchorage. A rotten hulk, with boards nailed over the windows even.'

'Poor Bagenal Harvey was hanged off Wexford Bridge and they made a football of his head through the streets. Dick Monk was shot dead by the yeos.'

'You seem to know a lot about them,' Charlie said.

'The whole country knows about them. They will be the subject of songs from now on. Their names will be on everyone's lips but it won't bring them back. Nor save the many who must leave Ireland to escape the same death.'

By now voices were raised in argument where Best was sitting with the others. 'I'll tell you about liberty,' Best was saying. 'Liberty is a full belly and a warm berth, that's my politics.'

'Man, you couldn't have it in Ireland. You'd have another man's foot on your belly.'

Best stood up and rolled back his sleeve. He held his right arm up to the light and Dónal saw the muscles stand out on it. 'There's no man would put his foot in my belly. See that? That arm would bring 'im down!'

The strangers murmured in agreement, and one of

them said, 'We have no quarrel with you, sailor. Only with your king.'

Best looked around to Charlie and Dónal. 'Nor I have no quarrel with you. My best mates are Irish, see.'

The strangers turned to look at them too.

The one who had asked Dónal his name said, 'Are you going back to your navy?'

The question shocked Dónal. 'Would you have us desert?' he replied. 'That would be dishonourable.'

'And where is the honour in fighting your country's allies? The French ship came here to aid Ireland. Now that you have attacked her, what hope is there for us?'

'That ship was only a trick,' Dónal replied, stung to the heart by the words. 'The real landing has taken place in Killalla!'

There was a stunned silence. Dónal received a secret kick from Charlie.

'Killalla, did you say? In the County Mayo?'

The group across the room broke into a lively discussion. The man sitting beside Charlie asked them if it was true.

Charlie said, "I'm not too sure he should have said it, but the truth of it is that General Humbert and a thousand men have landed at Killalla. They have taken Castlebar.' He thought to himself that they would know this by tomorrow or the day after anyway.

The man stood up. 'I am obliged to you for the information. Maybe there's hope yet.'

Charlie stood up too and offered him his hand. 'Good luck to you. But I do not think you'll win this fight. Napoleon is too busy to care for the likes of Ireland. A thousand French would man no more than two first-rate ships of the line. He'll never take the country with that.'

'We'll see, my friend. Now go back to your ship before the watch comes upon ye. They're out all night these times.'

It was only then Dónal noticed that the fat landlord had vanished.

They found the boat where they had left it and slid it quietly down into the water. The tide was ebbing now and carried them swiftly downriver even before they pulled on the oars. Charlie and Best rowed and Dónal sat in the stern, thinking about the conversation they had had with the men in the tavern.

The question that the stranger had put to him, about leaving the ship, had shocked him. By now, after only two months on board, he had grown to love the ship. He respected the captain. He had fought a battle and been on the winning side. His friends were there. It was unthinkable that he should leave her. Yet the question bothered him. *Where was the honour in fighting his country's allies?* The French ship had not set out to attack Ireland. She was sent as a trick to occupy the blockade, so that General Humbert and his men could get though to help drive the English out. And he, Dónal Long, had helped to capture her.

They were drawing closer to the *Leander* and the oars dipped slowly and silently. Ahead of him, Dónal saw the ship that had been his home since the time he ran away. He realised, with a start, that he was a sailor now, as he had always wished to be, and it was not as simple as he had thought.

The tide was stronger than they expected and the jolly boat struck the ship's sides with a loud thump. They fended her off as best they could while Best tied her rope off to the captain's stern gallery. Then they let her glide down the ship's side as far as the first gun port of the lower deck. Most of the gun ports were slightly open for air and this one was no exception. They lifted the hatch and one after the other slipped quietly in.

'Hsst,' a voice said.

'Who's that?' whispered Charlie.

'Me. Come here, Charlie Madden'.

Charlie stood up beside one of the hammocks. Out of it the ship's carpenter raised his white, toothless head.

'Watch out for squalls, Charlie Madden. Old Wilson was down 'ere 'bout three hours ago. 'Ad a good shove round your 'ammock. And the boy's. Shouldn't be s'prised if he knows you were out.'

'Thanks, John Fly. I won't forget it.'

They made their way back to the hammocks. 'Be careful in the morning, Dónal,' said Charlie. 'Say we went for drink. Don't mention talking to anyone. I'll be flogged for it and so will Besty. I shouldn't think they'll do much to you. Say we led you astray.'

Captain Somerville noted with satisfaction that Madden, Best and the boy had returned with the jolly boat. He too had observed their departure – the jolly boat floated directly under his stern windows. It was what he expected but he was pleased just the same. Twenty of his crew were Irish and any one of them might have taken it into his head to jump ship in a worrying time like this. It made for a good ship if the men could get away with the occasional breach of discipline. A good ship and a happy ship. If the men were happy the ship would be a better fighting weapon – it was as simple as that.

He would turn a blind eye to this bit of foolishness.

No doubt they would have all the stories of the rebellion. Rumours would fly around the decks. The men would become troublesome if they were kept here at anchor for too long. He hoped orders would come tomorrow to haul up to Waterford. There they could repair the masts and be fit to put to sea again in a matter of days.

Yes, he thought as he drifted to sleep, he was glad that the boy had returned. And he was glad that damned Wilson was not on watch when they returned. The fellow seemed to have taken a particular hatred of the boy.

'Beat to divisions.' Mr Wilson gave the order and the drum rolled out. It was morning and the men came sullenly from every point of the ship and assembled in their divisions facing the quarterdeck. Captain Somerville surveyed them as they arrived and observed that they were proving the old saying that harbours rot ships and ruin men. They were two nights at anchor and already they were becoming sullen, sulky and restless. Of course, none of them liked the idea of what was going on ashore. No doubt they thought about their own homes, those who had them, when they saw the burning villages. The sooner he had his masts repaired and the ship out of here the better for all hands.

'Carry on, Mr Wilson.'

Now the divisions began to report. 'All hands present and sober, sir.' One by one they answered the call. Mr

Wilson stood impassive at the quarterdeck rail. But when it came to Madden's division he stopped the reporting.

'Did you report all hands present, Mr Allen?'

'Yes, sir. All hands present and sober, sir.'

'Now that is a strange thing,' said Mr Wilson. 'Madden and Long stand forward.' Dónal and Charlie Madden stood forward. 'You were not in your hammock last night, Madden.'

Madden winked at the nearest man. 'No sir.' The crew all knew where Madden had been but they assumed that, like themselves, he simply wanted to go ashore after the long voyage and taste real beer and see some pretty girls. There was not one of them who had not been planning how they might get ashore too.

Mr Wilson's stony voice broke into their thoughts. 'In fact you left the ship in the jolly boat.'

'I'm sorry to say I did, sir. And I regret it now, sir, I have that sore a head, sir.' Laughter among the divisions.

'Silence there!' Wilson glared about him. Someone tittered and was hushed immediately. They were becoming a little uneasy. Old Wilson was making too much of this. Sailors were always sneaking ashore. The ordinary seaman considered it part of his duty to outwit his officers in trivial matters of discipline, while not one of them would leave his place at a gun or refuse to climb the rigging in a storm.

Wilson swung round to face the captain, his face a livid red. 'Captain Somerville, sir, I have to report that bosun Madden and the boy Long left the ship during the hours of darkness and went ashore. I suspect they may have attempted to make contact with the rebels, sir.'

There was a gasp of disbelief among the divisions. Not for the first time Captain Somerville was appalled by the behaviour of his first officer. If Wilson suspected something like this he should have come to him privately. It would not have taken long to make enquiries and the captain was sure that whatever happened ashore, Madden was no traitor to his comrades or his captain. At any rate, because Wilson had said what he said in public, before the men and the other officers, he would have to act now. There was no turning a blind eye on this one.

He stepped forward to the quarterdeck rail. 'What do you say, Madden? Did you attempt to make contact with the rebels?'

There was no laughter now. A deadly silence had fallen on the ranks of assembled men.

Madden cleared his throat and replied that he understood that the rebels had been put to flight. 'I went ashore, sir, this being my native land, as you might say. And because I longed for a glass of good Irish ale, what I haven't tasted this three months since we left the Cove of Cork last time, sir. I confess I brought the boy along for company. I led him astray, sir.'

'Very well, Madden. You will receive twelve lashes at four bells in the afternoon watch.' Again there was a gasp of disbelief. Twelve lashes was the maximum that naval law allowed, and although most captains took no notice of the law no one had ever heard Captain Somerville order twelve lashes before.

Nevertheless, Captain Somerville could see that Wilson was disappointed with the sentence. He fixed a steely eye on his first officer. 'Carry on, Mr Wilson.'

Wilson would not give in. Was the man a fool? 'But, Captain, this is treason he is charged with.'

Captain Somerville nodded to Wilson to walk with him and the two paced along the quarterdeck, talking quietly for some minutes. When they returned Captain Somerville spoke to the men.

'These are dangerous and disturbed times. Now my lads, we must all take care that we do not put ourselves in jeopardy. Mr Wilson has pointed out to me the seriousness of this charge. He maintains to me that we have only your word, Madden, that you did not speak to the rebels and perhaps betray our ship.'

Cries of 'No!' and 'Never Charlie Madden!' from the men. Captain Somerville knew they were right, but Wilson had forced him to this point, quite cleverly, and naval law did not allow him to let it pass.

He raised his hand. 'Certainly I would be surprised if you did such a thing, Madden and I declare I will speak in your favour at your court martial. Nevertheless, Mr Wilson insists I would not be doing my duty if I did not put you in chains. I will set a court martial in train as soon as we return to the Cove of Cork. I make no doubt that it will clear your name. Have you anything to say?' Charlie Madden shook his head. Mr Wilson was obviously jubilant. In such troubled times an Admiralty court martial was far more likely to hang Madden just in case than it was to turn him loose and clear his name.

A voice came from the divisions, a quiet voice that almost went unnoticed. '*I* have, Captain.' It was Best.

The captain almost smiled with relief. 'Yes, Best?'

'I was with him, sir. As I am an Englishman, I swear

he never betrayed the ship.'

Wilson was taken aback. 'You were with him?'

'I was, sir, there and back. And ship's carpenter John Fly will witness that he saw me come in the first larboard gun port on the lower deck along of the other two.'

Again Wilson and the captain paced the deck.

'Very well, Best,' said Captain Somerville. 'You and Madden will both receive twelve lashes at four bells in the afternoon watch. Carry on divisions.'

The matter seemed to be over. The divisions continued reporting and when they were finished Mr Wilson dismissed them. Captain Somerville went below to prepare a letter of request to be carried up by boat to the timber merchant who supplied oak for the masts. Madden was helping the carpenter to hold a plank in place when he was called aside by Mr Wilson.

'Mr Madden, when we reach Cove again I shall prosecute you before the Admiralty Court there. Not even the favouritism of Captain Somerville can save you from that. And mark me, in the present state of Ireland, the Admiralty will not look kindly on you. I promise you, as I live, that you will swing from a yardarm.'

Charlie Madden tipped his forelock mockingly. 'Sure your honour knows best,' he said. 'If it is my duty to swing then swing I will.' He had a strong feeling that Wilson would have killed him there and then if he had had a weapon.

9

'ALL HANDS TO WITNESS PUNISHMENT'

The flogging of Madden and Best was something that Dónal would always wish he had not seen. When the sentence of twelve lashes had been passed his heart was gladdened – twelve lashes of his uncle's belt would have been an easy thing to bear. He had heard about the cat-o'-nine-tails, but had never imagined that it would be as terrible as it proved to be. But the order *All hands to witness punishment* sent a wave of depression through the rest of the ship. The crew assembled on deck in absolute silence. Dónal was appalled by the spectacle, particularly by the sight of the bosun who gave the lashes, cleaning skin and blood off the strings between strokes. By the time the flogging was over both men had their backs stripped raw by the cat. Best was unconscious and Madden was raving. The surgeon had rubbed salt into the wounds to 'cure' them as he said, and the agony of that was as bad as the original flogging.

Afterwards, Best and Madden told Dónal that they had never been flogged before, although they had seen it done. Together they swore undying hatred for the man who had brought it on them. 'I'll kill that Wilson, yet,' Best declared. 'It'll be over the side some night when the wind is up. If I can get him off the quarterdeck, that is.'

In two days they received orders to haul up to the anchorage under Waterford Island where the repairs could be carried out, the timbers brought in a barge. The job of hauling the two ships up took a whole day, with all the ship's boats out to tow them. Now they were anchored within sight of the prison ship, a rotten old hulk with no masts and all her gun ports nailed shut.

Best and Madden soon saw that one of the sailors on the prison ship was an old shipmate who had lost a leg in an explosion. They hailed him, and over the days that followed, as the repairs slowly went ahead, there was a certain amount of traffic going secretly backwards and forwards, because orders were that no one was to go aboard the prison ship.

It was when Madden returned from the hulk one night that he told Dónal he had some news for him. 'There's one of your own people on that hulk. It's your uncle. The one you near poisoned. He was taken up as a United Irishman and there he lies in that miserable tub of rot.'

Dónal was so surprised that he had to sit down. His uncle? In the hulk awaiting transportation to Australia?

Madden explained how he had found out. The bosun on that rotten tub was an old shipmate of his, as Dónal knew. And as Dónal knew, Madden and Best had gone over a few nights for a chinwag. Besides, the food on the hulk was better than they had themselves and there was a plentiful supply of whiskey. One night the old bosun told him that there was a prisoner with a message for a lad on the *Leander*, and who should that prisoner be but Dónal's wicked uncle. The man had asked for a piece of paper and a quill and ink, which the bosun of the hulk had provided out of the kindness of his heart, and his uncle had written something down for him, which neither Madden nor the bosun could read, of course.

'Now how do you think that uncle of yours found out you was aboard, Dónal? Someone got word to him, that's for sure. Do you think it might be someone from that tavern?'

Dónal shook his puzzled head.

'Look, this is the letter.' Dónal took it eagerly and read it over twice, as it was difficult to decipher the scrawled letters.

My dear nefew

I confesse I gev you up for lost after I came back the Night of the bad Wisky. I am right glad you were nott. How I cem to be in this Place I will not rite of. That is best forgot. I cem to this Shippe on the 10th day of Julie, as I remember, & have been here under sentance of Trasportation since. Times look black. There is nere five hundred Men here now. The Sicknesse & the Filt is a tarrible thing to behold. We are not permitted to see the Light of Day above once in the Weke. Manys a time I wisht you & me was back in the little Cottage & the happy Days. Do not hate me for what I done to you. I will never see Ireland again.

Pray for Michael Long

'I must go to see him, Charlie.'

'It cannot be, Dónal, a stór. Think what would happen if you were caught? This time what excuse would you have? If they caught you talkin' to a rebel prisoner, no matter that he is your uncle, there would be no saving you. I cannot help you to do that.'

Dónal was not satisfied. 'If you won't aid me, Charlie, I'll have to do it myself.'

But the chance made itself.

Captain Somerville observed that the men were near mutinous and he did not blame them. Those who were British had no quarrel with the United Irishmen. As far as they were concerned they had been given a job to do to capture this Frenchman and they had done it. They had fought hard and won. The port authorities were landsmen one and all, in the opinion of the sailors, so not worth a pinch of salt, and now they were keeping the *Leander* anchored off with no shore leave, when the sailors should have been touring the waterfront taverns and drinking their pay. They did not like it.

Those who were Irish were disturbed by the signs they had seen. They imagined their homes destroyed, the hated yeomen roaming the countryside. Not one of them would leave his post in battle but here in the rotten quiet of the anchorage many were thinking of deserting ship.

Captain Somerville was beginning to lose patience with the port authorities. He had the discipline of his ship to think about; they had the running of their port. The sooner the *Leander* was repaired and provisioned and on the high seas again, the happier everyone would be. He was beginning to think of hauling the ship up to the quay himself.

The work was finished and the barge was pulling away when the port captain's launch was seen falling down towards them on the ebb tide. Mr Wilson turned out a welcoming party for a man of such standing and the bosun played his pipe to signal his arrival. All this formality was new to Dónal and he had to be told that it was the right way to behave. The port captain's launch drew smartly alongside and a man in a neat uniform stepped off and climbed aboard the *Leander*.

'Captain Somerville's compliments and would you join him in his day cabin, sir?'

'Lead the way, Lieutenant.'

Wilson and the port captain went below and were there for almost an hour. Everyone knew what the port captain was there for. In the meantime, Best, chatting through the open gun port with the men in the launch, learned as much as the captain did in his cabin.

They were to ship a load of prisoners and take them to Cove. There the prisoners would be transferred to a transport that would take them to Australia. There they be would sold as indentured servants – literally slaves – of the planters, and serve out their sentences.

'So now,' said Charlie Madden, in a temper about it, 'we're going to be gaolers as well! That's not sailors' work!'

But Dónal's mind was racing ahead. What if his uncle was one of the prisoners? What if he should find a chance to free him? What then?

That was where his thinking stopped. The consequence of any attempt to free his uncle meant escape from the *Leander*. It meant leaving his friends and deserting the ship. Could he do it? Where did his loyalty lie? At any rate he would soon find out.

By evening they were tied up alongside the quay. Captain Somerville had passed the order that the starboard watch could have shore leave that night, larboard watch tomorrow. He did not expect they would be in Waterford a third night.

The men of the starboard watch prepared themselves for the evening out with extraordinary care, to Dónal's eyes. Most of the sailors had long hair and they plaited this into pigtails, of which they were extremely proud. They wore their best shirt, if they had one, and begged one from their friends if they hadn't. Some of them had shoes, though they never wore shoes on board, even in the worst weather, because they said shoes made your feet slip. They went down the gangplank to the quay with delight in their eyes, and several hours later they were dragged back on board by the bosuns of the starboard watch, much the worse for the strong liquor they had consumed and many of them bruised from fighting. When they came to in the morning they all reckoned it had been a great night and recounted tales of the enormous quantities of beer or rum or whiskey they had consumed, the beautiful girls they had met and the heroic fights they had taken part in.

About seven bells in the forenoon watch the prisoners were led aboard. They came down the quay in chains, twenty of them, followed by a silent crowd of townspeople and countryfolk. Some of them were well dressed and obviously well-off farmers or professional people, but most of them were ragged and poverty stricken. All of them had a haggard, grey look as a result of their time on the prison ship. They shuffled along, manacled at hand and foot, driven by a company of soldiers with fixed bayonets.

Dónal's uncle was the fifth man to come up the gangplank. He passed Dónal with only a glance so that Dónal did not know whether he had seen him or not.

The prisoners were led forward and stood in a disconsolate group around the base of the mainmast. The officer who had brought them handed some papers to Captain Somerville, saluted and left with his men. Captain Somerville surveyed the prisoners.

'You men,' he said, 'have been kept in the prison ship for some time. I will have you know that this is a ship of war. Absolute discipline prevails here. Once you step on board my ship you become subject to that discipline. Any breach of that discipline will result in immediate punishment. However, you will not be confined below decks, as I understand you have been until now. You will be allowed on deck for a portion of each day. Below decks, you will be confined, but your quarters will be properly aired and you will receive the same rations as the sailors. My duty is to bring you safe to Cork. After that your safety will pass out of my hands. I do not intend to lose as much as one of you until then. We will set sail tomorrow on the high tide.'

To Captain Somerville's consternation the port captain was aboard again within the hour. The roads, he said, were dangerous due to the recent insurrection, and a party of ladies wishing to go to Cork would arrive from Lord Beresford's estate within a day at most. The port captain earnestly wished Captain Somerville to convey these ladies to Cork, if it would not be too great an imposition.

'It is an appalling imposition on a fighting ship, sir, altogether too much to bear! Convicts and women all together! Properly speaking there is no place for either on a man-of-war!'

The port captain pleaded and in the end, Captain Somerville agreed. It meant a wait of at least one more day.

Another visitor to the ship.

The man announced himself as Edward Roche of Killinarden, brother of one of the prisoners. He begged Captain Somerville to allow him to see his brother one more time. His brother was under sentence of transportation, indeed had narrowly escaped hanging, and Edward Roche did not expect to see him again in life. A farewell, a word of forgiveness were all that he sought. He would give his word of honour not to interfere in any way.

Captain Somerville agreed.

Mr Wilson visited Captain Somerville in his cabin. 'May I have your permission to go ashore, sir? There are some matters of a private nature I must attend to.'

Captain Somerville agreed. 'Be so good as to repair aboard again by eight bells, Mr Wilson.'

A wine merchant called in the first dogwatch, an enormously fat man. He had several samples of his wine and urged Captain Somerville to purchase some as he would surely be entertaining guests on his return to Cork. Captain Somerville replied that he would purchase his wines from Woodford's on his return to Cork, as they had always provided him in the past. The wine merchant informed him that his first officer, Mr Wilson, had already purchased a quantity of the very best quality.

Captain Somerville was not surprised that Mr Wilson had purchased wine, as all officers had to provide what luxuries they required for themselves. What did surprise him was what this fat wine merchant next saw fit to tell him.

Captain Somerville was beginning to wish they were out at anchor again, where there would be fewer callers to interfere with the smooth running of his ship.

Mr Wilson came aboard promptly at eight bells.

Lord Beresford's women did not arrive next day. But two men of the larboard watch deserted after their shore leave. One was recovered by the bosun, blind drunk in a back street. The other was suspected of having shipped aboard a merchant brig bound for Bristol. Captain Somerville knew that if they were delayed much longer there would be further desertions. He agreed with the port captain that he would wait a further day.

Darkness was falling earlier and earlier now as September went on. The weather was still fine and warm but the nights were colder. Mr Wilson in his boat cloak looked an altogether bigger figure than Mr Wilson in just his uniform. He towered over Dónal, who was sitting on the gunwale, staring at the magical lights reflected in the water from across the river, and wondering what was to become of himself and his uncle. So intent on the lights was he that the officer's voice almost startled him into the river.

'Tell Madden I want him.'

'Aye aye, sir.' He scampered down to the lower gun deck where Charlie Madden was playing cards across his gun with three men from the middle deck. 'Old Wilson wants you topsides, Charlie.'

'Righto, mate.'

Charlie passed his cards on to Dónal, took up his jacket and hat and went out into the night air.

When the crew formed up in its divisions next morning, Charlie Madden was not there. He was brought aboard again before supper and carried straight down to the surgeon. Dónal was not permitted to see him. According to the men who brought him back he looked like he had been in a fight. They had found him near the church in Lady Lane, lying in a pool of blood. Dónal was frightened but he knew Charlie Madden's great heart and enormous strength.

But Charlie Madden died just before eight bells in the middle watch. Day dawned cold and unforgiving on the men of *Leander*, and Dónal's heart was the coldest of all.

10

A YEOMAN COLONEL

Later that day, Mr Wilson brought on board the *Leander* a man who styled himself Colonel Thomas Turner of the West Waterford Yeoman Cavalry, a tall red-faced man, who gave every evidence of preferring the back of a horse to the quarterdeck of a man-of-war.

'This gentleman,' Wilson was saying, 'will testify to you that Madden, Best and the boy were ashore on that night, that they visited a tavern frequented by rebels, that they spoke to some men known to be of the rebel persuasion and that they and the rebels seemed to be on friendly terms.'

Captain Somerville laughed outright.

'How will he testify to this, Mr Wilson? Is it a guessing game? Or was he actually present when this meeting took place? I can hardly believe these famous rebels and my men would bare their hearts in the presence of a Colonel of the yeos!'

'The truth, sir,' the yeoman said, 'is that I have an informant in that very tavern. Mr Deasy. A decent, loyal man.'

'Loyal,' said Captain Somerville, 'is hardly the word I would use for an informer.'

'I meant loyal to the crown.'

'I shall have to speak to this informer,' said Captain Somerville. 'I can hardly accept hearsay from a yeoman cavalry officer.'

The yeoman snapped upright. 'Are you questioning my honour, sir? Because if so I would have to demand satisfaction.'

'Oh, not your *honour*, Colonel,' he said. 'I know nothing of your honour. It is simply that I can take no action without directly questioning the witness myself.'

'All I ask, sir,' replied the yeoman, 'is that you hand the culprits over to my charge. I will undertake to have them tried before the military tribunal. The tribunal will consider all the evidence. It is the law of the land.'

'And I am the law on this ship in which these men serve. We do not use torture to extract confessions here. If the evidence is sufficient I will punish the men myself. And by the way, one of the men you accuse was killed last night while ashore, presumably under the protection of your law. I should like you to enquire of your informers who his murderers were.'

As he took his leave of the officers, it was clear from the look on the face of Colonel Thomas Turner of the West Waterford Yeoman Cavalry that he had no intention of searching for the murderers of a mere sailor.

Captain Somerville turned angrily to the lieutenant. 'Now, Mr Wilson, be so good as to explain how you came by this information, not to mention this yeoman.'

'Colonel Turner came on board one day while we were

still at anchor and had the timber-merchant's barge alongside. He was making enquiries concerning the activities of a party of notorious rebels. It was not difficult, given the information that he and I had, to put two and two together. I met Mr Deasy yesterday whilst I was ashore. Captain Turner arranged it.'

'You did not think fit to inform your captain?'

'I thought,' said Mr Wilson carefully, 'that you were a trifle overburdened with the repairs. I thought I would carry out the enquiries myself and perhaps rise in your esteem if I could solve the problem,'

'Look here, Mr Wilson. This business between you and Madden. Something got between you and the wind there, I know that. Now I don't want to know what Madden did to you or you did to Madden but the man is dead, what. What can you gain by persecuting the boy? And Best? Best is an Englishman through and through. Do you seriously think he was aiding the rebels?'

Mr Wilson was enjoying the spectacle of Captain Somerville pleading with *him.* 'We believe he may have become infected with the revolutionary doctrines by association with Madden and the boy.'

Captain Somerville was astounded. 'Revolutionary doctrines? Why, the men are illiterate. They could not spell 'doctrine'. You go too far, sir.'

'The boy, as you know, Captain, can read and write. As a matter of fact he has some little Latin and possibly Greek. It is certain he can read English. There is further evidence which you shall hear when Colonel Turner returns with his witness.'

Captain Somerville took a deep breath. He would

explain to Mr Wilson, just once more, how important it was for an officer to have the trust of his men, how an officer should never display petty hatreds or favouritism, how he should hold his head up and remain aloof from the squabbles of the between-decks. He was not a great talker and he hoped he could find the right words to say what he wanted to say. He had little hope that Mr Wilson would understand, but he would say it once more because he felt he had a duty to try to make an officer of the man.

'Mr Wilson, you and I are officers of His Majesty's Royal Navy. You and I know that on board of a man-of-war a great deal must pass unnoticed. The unity of shipboard life is everything. Everything, sir. That is why the men never steal from one another. Because they all depend one upon another. We officers also depend upon our men and they on us. By continuing this quarrel, you disturb that unity. Wait until the *Leander* is at sea again and the clean fresh air will wash away all this foolishness.' Captain Somerville could almost smell the beautiful sea air as he spoke. 'The sea is the great cleanser. And a good set-to with the enemy, broadside and broadside. Nothing like it to lift the heart and clear the head, what! I pray God to be at sea again and to come up with some Frenchman. You should pray for it too, sir. You will feel better for it. All of this will be as nothing.'

Mr Wilson smirked. 'I feel bound to tell you, Captain Somerville, that I have applied to their lordships of the Admiralty for a new posting. I will be leaving the *Leander*, I hope, at Cork.'

So that was it. He was jumping ship at Cork. Looking forward to a new ship, away from his tiresome Irish captain. And now, on the last leg of the voyage he was settling his old scores. Be damned to the man! If that was the lay of it, the captain would tell him to his face what he thought of him!

'I hope you do not expect a good report from me, Mr Wilson. A less dignified officer it has never been my misfortune to sail with! In my opinion you are not fit to command men. Any captain would be foolish to take you aboard!'

They parted on those terms.

It was open warfare now and Captain Somerville realised that it would take all his skill to save the lives of the two remaining accused. Best stood a better chance, being English. But how to protect the boy Dónal?

If only they had their orders and could put to sea.

Captain Somerville was surprised to find out that he had already met Mr Wilson's witness. The lieutenant stood before him again in his day cabin. With him were Colonel Turner, the yeoman, and the fat wine merchant who had pressed him to buy wine the day before. The wine merchant was explaining how he had noticed the connection between the rebels and members of the crew of the *Leander*.

Two men and a boy had come into his tavern shortly after one o'clock on the night in question, he said. He, the wine merchant, had taken particular notice of it because the hour was so late and because none of the sailors in the merchant ships were, at that time, venturing out after dark. As soon as he had served them their ale, and a glass of milk for the boy, they had struck up a conversation with the other customers. These customers were known to the wine merchant as supporters of the United Irishmen. He had not overheard their conversation because he slipped out to send a message to Colonel Turner by his serving boy. He was delayed some little time in writing the message and when he returned the three sailors had gone. Not long afterwards Colonel Turner and a party of yeomen arrived and some shooting occurred, which caused considerable damage to his premises, and resulted in the death of two men – one of the rebels and one of the yeomen. In the confusion the other men evaded capture. As a consequence he was in fear of his life and Colonel Turner had very kindly posted two of his men to guard the tavern and escort the wine merchant around the town.

'But this is nothing,' Captain Somerville said. It was quite likely that the three sailors had no idea the men they were talking to were troublemakers.

'But that is not all,' Mr Wilson continued. The wine merchant had overheard one other significant fact. He licked his lips and glanced nervously at Colonel Turner.

'On my return I heard one of the rebels say that the boy was the nephew of one Michael Long, a rebel. I distinctly heard him say ... '

Colonel Turner interrupted. 'Michael Long was taken after Vinegar Hill, having been in the company of the notorious Popish priest John Murphy. He was tortured but would not reveal the whereabouts of Murphy. Murphy is still at large and there is a considerable reward on his head.'

'And you would like that reward, what, Colonel?' Somerville was smiling but it was a cold smile. 'You would like your prize money?'

Turner's face was a livid red. With an effort he controlled his words. 'I should like to do my duty and bring those who rebelled against His Majesty before the military tribunal. I request that you hand the man Best and the boy Long over to me.'

Captain Somerville turned his back on them and walked to the windows that looked out over the stern. There was no comfort there. Instead of the wide, clean sea and the white waves of the ship's wake, his windows simply looked out on the bows of another ship, a grubby coal boat, filthy from stem to stern and crewed by good-for-nothings.

He turned again and walked to the door of the cabin. He opened it wide enough to see the face of the marine sentry outside.

'Master-at-arms, bring up the boy Dónal Long.' The master-at-arms saluted and tramped off.

An uneasy silence fell on the cabin until there was a tap at the door and Dónal entered, haggard and pale.

'Long, these men have made certain accusations against you.' Dónal looked at his accusers and shivered when he recognised the face of the man who had served him milk in the tavern on the quay.

'They claim you are the nephew of one Michael Long? Is that so?'

Dónal remembered that telling the truth to the captain had helped him before. 'I am, sir. Michael Long is the uncle I have so often told you about.'

Captain Somerville smiled. 'The one you poisoned with the porridge, is it?'

'The very one, sir. But he has been in trouble since. I have spoken to him since he was brought aboard and he tells me he has been in the insurrection, sir. They have tortured him horribly. He is a broken man, with the sight of only one eye, and the fingers of the one hand useless. He will never be able to work again.'

Captain Somerville swallowed hard. Dónal was in great danger now, and he must choose his words with the greatest care to save the young boy from falling into the hands of Turner and his yeomen, who would torture him like his uncle.

'Tell me now, Long, you had not been in communication with your uncle before he came aboard this ship, had you?' Turning to the others he said – 'I allow the men to speak to the prisoners since they came aboard, you see. The boy cannot be blamed for speaking to his uncle, since I have allowed it by direct orders.'

Dónal wondered at the way the question was put. Could it be that Captain Somerville wanted him to say no? But the letter he had in his breeches pocket was surely a harmless one. If he were to show it, openly and honestly, would it not be better for himself? And since his uncle had expressed contrition in the note and asked for his prayers, would it not be better for his uncle too?

Turner snatched the letter before Dónal could pass it to the captain. He and Wilson and the fat man read it with eager eyes. Finally Turner looked up triumphantly.

'Proof, Captain Somerville? What more proof could you need? He gives here the exact number of prisoners held on the ship and information concerning their exercise above deck.'

Mr Wilson added, 'With this information the Irish could mount an attack on the prison ship and liberate five hundred of their worst rebels. The boy must be handed over!'

Captain Somerville looked from Dónal to the letter to Mr Wilson in dismay.

The port captain was waiting his turn outside the cabin door as Colonel Turner marched Dónal back on deck. He was about to enter Captain Somerville's cabin when he was almost knocked to the floor by flabby Mr Deasy the tavern keeper who was hastily leaving the room, followed by the first officer, Mr Wilson. That's a funny chap to have aboard, he thought.

He knocked and was surprised at the harshness of the captain's voice calling him in. Somerville was standing with his back to him, gazing out his stern gallery at the coal boat unloading. He turned, saw that his next guest was the port captain and immediately excused himself for not greeting him.

'I am troubled by matters of discipline, Port Captain. A ship at sea is a very much healthier and happier place. Ships are troubled being near the land. They do not like it, nor do their crew. I hope you have good news for me?'

The port captain beamed. 'Indeed I do, Captain. Great news indeed. Lord Beresford's ladies appear after all to have made their way to Cork by carriage. They are hourly expected there, having left Youghal this morning by post-chaise. They apparently left Lord Beresford's estate three days ago but his Lordship neglected to inform me.'

Captain Somerville struggled to smile at the port

captain. 'In that case, Port Captain, I trust you have my sailing orders with you?'

Again the port captain beamed. 'You are to sail on the next tide. Bound for the Cove of Cork. Discharge your prisoners. Take on provisions. Thence to cruise south to Biscay, where I am assured there are French ships in plenty and prizes for the taking.'

Now it was Captain Somerville's turn to beam. 'The next tide? Let me see? Less than four hours to be ready. I must make haste.'

'But you are ready to put to sea this past three days, Captain?'

'Indeed, indeed. You are quite right. You will have a glass of wine with me, Port Captain?'

The port captain beamed even more as the wine flowed. He smacked his lips at the first taste. 'You did not purchase this wine from Mr Deasy, our wine merchant and tavern-keeper.'

'That scoundrel,' said Captain Somerville. 'The man is not to be trusted with a glass of water.'

'Indeed, Captain, he sells a scurvy wine. Not to be tasted, let alone purchased. I confess I was surprised to see him in your cabin.'

'Not so surprised as I was, I assure you,' was Captain Somerville's reply.

11

THE PRISON VAN

It was to the guardhouse where I was led,
and in the guardhouse where I was tried,
My sentence passed and my courage low
To Geneva Barracks I was forced to go.

Dónal found himself in a crowded guardhouse set into
what looked like the remains of a huge wall. So far as he
could judge by the groaning and weeping, there were at
least thirty people there. The place stank so badly it was
difficult to breathe. The evening light through the small
window was dying. Night was coming down.

He had been marched here under armed escort without
being given time to say goodbye to his friends or his
uncle. Turner took his father's knife from him and said
that it would make 'useful evidence'. As he passed
through the narrow streets the people were amazed to see
a young boy guarded by four armed yeomen and their
officer. After a time, the usual crowd that followed the
yeomen had collected. Countrymen in coarse cloth with
high hats and ashplants for walking sticks, women and

girls in black cloaks or red petticoats, their heads bare
or shawled, townspeople coming out of the lanes, even a
priest – they walked in his footsteps and followed him
to the guardhouse. One of the girls who had followed him
from the quay gasped aloud when she saw where he was
going. Another cried, 'God bless you, boy.' When they got
to the guardhouse gate, two of the yeomen turned and
faced the crowd, muskets at the ready. The yeoman
captain hammered on the door, and before long Dónal
heard the gaoler coming and the keys rattling in the lock.

The door swung open and he stepped into a small
courtyard. The gaoler opened the door in what looked like
the city wall and Dónal was pushed in. Darkness fell on
him immediately, a darkness that seemed complete until
Dónal looked up and saw the barred window high up in
the room. That was when he noticed that it was evening.

Time wore slowly along in the guardroom and Dónal's
eyes did not become accustomed to the gloom. He could
make out vague shapes at times, or detect slight move-
ments. Hours seemed to pass, though how many he could
not know. He knew there were people near him.

A voice spoke to him. 'I'm blind.'

'It's very dark,' Dónal said. 'But we'll maybe have the
moonlight later on.'

His reply seemed to infuriate the speaker, who grasped
his arm and squeezed so hard that Dónal cried out.

'I'm blind! Blind! Don't tell me about the moon!'

Dónal begged his pardon.

'Blinded by false fire, I was.'

Dónal said he was sorry to hear it.

'That oul' musket! I should a' thrown it away. The flash

went off in the pan. Threw the fire back in me eyes instead of out the barrel. If only I had a kept one eye closed, I'd have the sight a one eye anyway!' Dónal agreed with the voice that it was a pity indeed. 'Never trust an oul musket! The pike is the man. Look! I'd drive it this way, see?' Dónal could not see, but he knew what a boarding pike was, and he could feel the blind man's bony hand against his ribs. 'God damn the yeos!' He began to shout. 'God damn the cowardly yeos!' He repeated this three or four times until they heard the gaoler approaching.

Dónal sat down with his back propped against the wall, hoping that he would hear no more from the blind rebel. Another voice spoke to him.

'What has you here?'

'I was taken up by Captain Turner, the yeoman.'

'God help you so.'

'I'm to be tried in Geneva Barracks.'

'Geneva Barracks? Geneva torture house is a better name for it. Give me your hand.' He guided Dónal's hand up over his face to the top of his head. He had no hair, and the skin had the peculiar dead feel of a burn. 'Do you feel that head? They tore my hair out and burned the skin with a candle.' Dónal's hand recoiled. 'Information they were wanting. I'd have given it to them if only I had it.'

'They'll take you up tonight.' Another voice from the darkness. 'That's how they do it. They'll move you after dark. Very quick, maybe out the door and into the carriage. Small party of yeomen or dragoons. Turner won't be there. He never stirs from his fireside at night. It's tomorrow you'll see him.'

Dónal said, 'You know a lot about it.'

'Don't ask him questions,' someone else said. 'He knows what he's saying.'

'If you have any information, tell them. It'll only be worse if you don't, and they'll get it out of you in the end. There's hundreds and thousands have passed through their hands in Wexford and Waterford alone.'

Dónal remembered the news the soldier had brought to Captain Somerville. 'But the French have landed. They landed in Killalla. There's hope yet for us.'

No one answered.

'There's hope yet,' he said again, not quite so sure that he had said the right thing.

'You haven't heard, so, wherever you were?' The new voice was more educated than the others. 'The French were defeated on the eighth day of September. Cornwallis had thirty thousand men against a thousand Frenchmen and another thousand badly armed Irish. Thirty thousand!'

So the French were defeated, as everyone on the *Leander* had expected. Captain Somerville and Mr Wilson would be pleased. They would cheer when they heard, that friendly naval cheering. Dónal wished he were there to hear it.

On board the *Leander* the crew was working hard. Boats had been launched to haul the ship out into the channel. Huge ropes stretched from the boats to the ship. The bowlines were taut. Topsails were ready, to be set and backed at the right moment to give the ship a little extra movement.

Slowly she was pulled out, with much heaving and hauling and the shouted chant of Thaddeus Gallahoo:

So long my boys you've kept the sea you cannot tie
a bowline,

Haul bowline, the bowline haul!

The ropes that kept her moored to the quay fell away one by one in an organised pattern. A few of the port captain's workers helped there. Along the quay was a small crowd of onlookers, the regular women and young girls who came to say farewell to Jack Tar, as they called their sailor friends. At one end of the quay a knot of about twenty men stood watching carefully from the shadows.

The huge ship inched out, swinging silently so that her head was slowly turning downstream. Then the order was given *'Mainsail haul!'* and the mainsail unfurled quickly from its yard and was braced around with much stamping and hauling until it caught the wind in its folds and the ship began to gather way. Now she was moving slowly downriver. The boats that had hauled her out came up alongside, rowing for all they were worth, and were tied off, the crew climbing aboard as if their friends meant to leave them in Waterford. Now Thaddeus Gallahoo was singing a new and joyful song, his wooden leg hopping off the deck in a sharp tattoo:

My name is Edward Hollander, as you may understand,

I was born in the city of Waterford in Erin'slovely
land,

I was 'prenticed to a butcher for three long years
or more

Till I shipped aboard the Erin's Queen, the pride of
Old Tramore

The crew went about their tasks with a will, certain that before long the ship would put her broad foot on the Atlantic and leave the surly land behind.

Instead of clearing harbour and setting sail on the night breeze for Cork, the *Leander* dropped her anchor in the old spot, just above Duncannon, a few miles downstream from Waterford. When the ship was secure Captain Somerville ordered Mr Wilson below. 'I'll take your watch,' said he. 'You've been exceedingly busy these past days. Get below out of my sight.'

The old ship, battle-scarred and troubled, lay quietly to her anchor in the darkness. Captain Somerville paced the quarterdeck, thinking of all that she had gone through and how a wall of oak, a keel and clouds of white sail made a ship; how the ship is made by men, shipwrights and sailmakers; and how over the years he had seen the ship, in turn, make the men, men such as Charlie Madden, Gunner Best, Thaddeus Gallahoo. Even he was a different person to the young Henry Somerville who had left west Cork so many years before to seek his fortune as a midshipman in the Navy. The ship had made Mr Wilson too, he supposed, though Captain Somerville could not find it in his heart to blame any ship for making Mr Wilson what he was.

Darkness had fallen and there was no moon to light up the small barred square over his head. Dónal dreaded the night to come. The voices said he would be brought to the barracks by night, and that made sense to avoid disturbances or in case of an attack. What then? Geneva Barracks? The torture chamber? What information could he give his torturers? That his father had been a United Irishman but was now dead? That his uncle had been a rebel and had fought against them, but was now a broken man, incapable of earning a living, much less being a threat to the forces of the Crown?

The forces of the Crown? What did that mean? What harm had his English friends done to him? None. Did the Navy have anything to do with this cruelty and torture that he saw all round him? It was hard to know who his people were. There was Mr Wilson, an Englishman and his enemy. But Mr Wilson was the enemy of Best as well, and Best was an Englishman too. Then there was Charlie Madden, poor dead Charlie Madden. And Captain Somerville was an Irishman and very proud of it. Yet he had sailed to Ireland to help prevent the rebellion succeeding. His ship was helping to keep the red-coated soldiers from even greater danger. His king was not Ireland's king. And then, the yeomen were Irish. They came from the countryside and knew the countryside. They mounted patrols and beat and tortured. And the fat wine merchant was an Irishman. He remembered how his father had quoted Wolf Tone: 'To unite the whole people of Ireland, to abolish the memory of past dissensions, to substitute the common name of Irishman . . . ' How, he wondered, could that ever happen?

Dónal's thoughts were interrupted by the sound of a carriage drawing up outside. At the sound, people began to groan in the darkness. The blind man began to sing a defiant ballad. The gaoler's keys turned in the lock. A lantern threw its light into the room and Dónal saw, for the first time, the bare stone walls, the mud floor and the battered and broken remains of the men whose voices he heard since he came.

'Right. Step out Long, Fitzgerald and Byrne. Step out at once.' A yeoman officer barked the order. It was not Turner, as the voices had predicted.

The three stepped blinking into the light, and were hustled into the prison van. The door slammed and Dónal was in darkness again. The carriage tilted as the guards climbed up, then a whip cracked and the horse's hooves clattered on the cobbled stones. He heard the yeoman telling the guards to take the Passage Road, and then they were moving.

Dónal was dimly aware of the presence of the other two men. He was startled when one whispered, close to his ear, 'You are a boy.' It was the educated man who had told him earlier about the defeat of General Humbert and his French landing force. 'Listen to me carefully. My name is not Byrne, as they think. My name is John Colclough. I am a United Irishman. There is a price on my head. They do not yet know who I am but it is only a matter of time.'

'Why are you telling me this?' Dónal hissed. Such information was deadly dangerous.

'They will torture you as they will me. Unless you give them something they will destroy you. Give them my name and you will be saved. You will be transported but at least you will have your health. Give them my name and they will spare you. My days are numbered anyway. Pray for the soul of John Colclough. '

Dónal was moved. This man was giving himself up to save a boy he had only just met. 'But I cannot do it,' Dónal said. 'I am not what you think. And I cannot betray you. You would not save me if you knew what I had done.'

The other man did not reply. The carriage rattled along over the cobbles, moving more slowly now through the narrow winding streets. Suddenly the horses clattered to a stop. Dónal heard shouting.

'Stand or we shoot!'

'Who goes there?'

'Put up your sword!'

There was the muffled sound of a body falling. The door of the prison van flew open. Men with pistols stood in the darkness outside. Some of them wore hats with a green cockade, the sign of the United Irishmen. The three prisoners tumbled out.

'Thank God, lads,' said John Colclough.

The men ignored him, but two of them, seizing Dónal's shoulders, all but lifted him off the ground. They made off into the darkness of the side streets in the direction of Passage and Geneva Barracks.

Those townspeople who were roused from their beds by the noise on the Passage Road witnessed the strangest event of that strange year. Twenty or so rebels had held up the prison van, the carriage in which the prisoners were transported to the barracks. They had detained the guards at pistol point and knocked the escorting yeomen smartly upon the head so that not one of them could get away to raise the cry. The three prisoners had been released from the prison van, one of them the young boy everyone had seen marched in earlier. Then, strangest of all, these United Irishmen had made off into the darkness at a fast run, two of them carrying the boy bodily along, completely ignoring the other two prisoners. The townspeople were amazed, and doubly amazed that these rebels had worn pigtails when everyone knew the rebels cropped their hair short – that was why they were called Croppies. And almost as amazing was that they had the very best false accents you could imagine. If you did not know they were rebels you would have taken them for low-born Englishmen from Liverpool or Bristol!

They halted to catch their breath. Dónal, who had been frozen with terror from the time he stepped off the van, had time now to look around him and the first thing he noticed was the pigtails. Sailors! he thought. He scanned the men's faces and even in the darkness he thought he recognised them. They were from the *Leander*.

'Look lively lads. Show a leg.' It was Best. They set off again at a trot, the sailors' breathing coming in short gasps.

'Besty, Besty is that you?' Dónal cried.

''Course it's me, matey. Look lively now. No time to talk.'

Eventually they passed through the riverside village of Passage East and came to a stony beach looking down the river towards Duncannon. One of the men lit a lantern and showed it briefly in the direction of the river. Then they sat down.

'Besty,' said Dónal, 'I thought I was dead. I didn't know who you were. I thought you were some torturers come to get me.'

Best laughed.

'You mean you wouldn't recognise an honest sailor lad?' All the men laughed. 'Did you think we came to kill you?'

'I don't know what I thought,' Dónal replied. 'But I did not expect to be rescued. How did you do it?'

'No time to talk, lad. I'll tell you the whole story when we're stowed below by my gun.'

Captain Somerville had observed the light flickering on the Waterford shore.

'Launch your boat, bosun.'

Two men overhauled the tackle and the boat dropped gently into the sea. Four men pulled it away and in a short time it had crossed to the other side. The men on deck held their breath. The dark mass of the boat left the shore again and they could see that more men were returning than went out. When it pulled alongside there were fourteen men in it. The first to come aboard was Dónal Long. As the boat put out again to pick up the others, the Captain put his fingers to his lips and led Dónal below into his cabin.

When they were inside he sat down and wiped his forehead. He pointed to his stern gallery window to where they could see the black shadow of the boat slipping back across the water again. 'No one hurt?' Dónal shook his head. 'I'll tell you what, the carpenter is waiting outside. He'll hide you while I think what to do. Slip out now. Wouldn't do for Mr Wilson to find you back aboard, would it?'

As Dónal went to the door he added, 'It was Best's

plan, my boy. We left Waterford without them – Best and the others. They went to find out what they could. Rescue you if possible. Return to the ship tonight without fail.'

'By the by, we sail at four bells.'

12

MR WILSON'S BARGAIN

The *Leander* was sailing like a tub. Captain Somerville was not happy with the repairs to the mast and he was taking the trip to Cork very gently. Because a ship of her size could not go close to the wind they had first sailed for most of a day due south, and now seemed to be sailing almost exactly back over their tracks. This was called 'beating'. The wind was south-west and as long as it stayed in that quarter, the sailors assured Dónal, they could beat up and down for days. The trip that took them only a day to make going east was going to take them two at least going west. During all this time Dónal must skulk between the decks and hide whenever Wilson came in sight. However the weather was fine and Dónal was, above all else, delighted to be still alive, with all his limbs and his five senses. He felt something of the sailor's joy in leaving the complications of the land behind. Out here everything seemed simpler, cleaner, newer. The sea sparkled in the autumn sunshine, the winds were mild. And he was making friends again with his uncle, not only a broken man but a changed one, who marvelled that

Dónal had escaped death in the violent storm of his second night at sea and also that he had miraculously escaped torture and death at the hands of the yeomanry of West Waterford.

Best had told him the whole story.

The sailors, according to Best, were all determined not to let *their* powder monkey fall into the hands of those murdering landlubbers so they organised a deputation to approach the captain. With Best at their head, Miller, a bosun of the larboard watch, ship's carpenter John Fly, Thaddeus Gallahoo, and other important men from between the decks, they presented a plan to Captain Somerville. Twenty men, hand-picked by Best, most of them of Irish origin, would remain ashore at Waterford Quay. Once the *Leander* was gone they would spread out among the drinking-shops and inns. They would be bound to pick up information. Once they knew where Dónal was kept they could at least attempt to free him.

Most of these men had been involved in such attempts before. Some had rescued shipmates from the hands of moneylenders, night watchmen and such like. Others had been involved in naval 'cutting out operations' where ships were stolen from the enemy, often in hand-to-hand fighting. And of course, in those times, many naval engagements were fought hand-to-hand anyway, so as not to damage the ships and lose some of the all important prize money. None of them had any misgivings about attacking a prison.

As it happened that was unnecessary. Within two hours the sailors knew where Dónal was, as did everyone in Waterford. They found out that the prisoners were usually moved at night in a prison van. Now the question for Best and his men was whether there would be time. The captain had left word that the ship would sail at four bells in the morning watch with or without his men. If they missed the boat they would have to make their own way to Cork and they certainly would not be safe travelling with an escaped prisoner.

Luck was on their side. They placed themselves in hiding on the road the prison van was known to take and saw it go down towards the prison. On its return they stepped out like common highwaymen and stuck their pistols in the faces of the escort.

'A few of the lads had belaying pins and they tapped the heads of them yeomen which made them come off their horses easy enough. We had you out and running before anyone knew what was up.'

Dónal could not thank them enough and they basked in his gratitude like cats in the sun.

'But Dónal, I'll tell you something that will surprise you.'

Here Best looked over his shoulder to see if the coast was clear. Four other sailors were listening to the tale and nodding their heads and they too looked about, nodding knowingly to each other.

'I'll tell you, Dónal. We know who killed our old mate Charlie Madden!'

Dónal was shocked. Since his arrest he had scarcely had time to think of Charlie except to wish he were still alive to help him as he had done before. Now the sorrow of his untimely death came flooding back. Tears welled up in his eyes and brimmed down his cheeks.

'Hark, lad. Do you want to know who done the deed?'
Again the careful look around. 'It were old Wilson, lad.
He paid two cut-throats to do the job for him and he sent
Charlie to his death up that lane.' His eyes narrowed. 'Every
crimp and thief in Waterford knows how it were done!'

Dónal's heart hardened into hatred. 'How will we kill
him, Besty?'

Best looked hard at Dónal. 'Dónal, lad, what I'm come
about to say to you is not easy. You are in trouble here.
The *Leander* is bound for Cove and that's a navy port. We
have our first officer here, old Wilson I mean, and he
won't let anything pass. You won't get off this ship unless
we play it canny now. We have to get to wind'ard of him
and I know how to do it.'

Captain Somerville was surprised to have a second
deputation of the men in his day cabin. 'What is it, my
lads? Are you not pleased with your bargain? You have
your powder monkey back. Do you want to be rid of him
again so soon?' He was enjoying himself hugely. He hadn't
yet thought of a way to steal the boy off the ship, but he
was certain that a way would show itself.

'We're right happy with our bargain as you calls it,
Captain,' Best replied. 'But we've come to tell you a bit
of bad news as we heard ashore in Waterford. Fact is,
Captain, we have found the murderer of Charlie Madden,
as these men can witness.'

He paused.

'Well, my man, spit it out!' Captain Somerville was
eager to hear the worst but already suspecting that he
knew.

'It's the first officer sir, the mate Mr Wilson. He planned it and he paid two cut-throats to do the work for him. Sullivan here had it directly from one of them, sir, and I regret to say Sullivan was unable to restrain himself from putting the same man in a bad way.'

'How bad a way, Sullivan?'

Sullivan had an unblinking stare and the calmest eyes Captain Somerville had ever seen. 'Matter o' fact, dead, sir.'

The Captain groaned. 'Witnesses?'

'Matter o' fact, sir, none, sir, as it fell out after dark, thanks be to God. And right close to the river, matter o' fact.'

'As it happens, sir, the boy Dónal has heard of this. Unhappily, sir, he means to do murder on Mr Wilson. For which he will surely swing from a yardarm, sir, and that'd be only right,' said Best.

'Matter o'fact,' said Sullivan, 'I'd do for him meself and be happy to swing for it!'

'That'll be enough, Sullivan,' Captain Somerville said. 'No mutiny on my ship or by God you'll all pay.'

Best looked sharply at his shipmate. 'Sullivan means no harm, Captain. But I have spoke to the boy, Dónal.' Somerville was amused by the formal way Best had begun to speak about his pet. 'I have a bargain to offer you, sir.'

Somerville replied that he had no need of a bargain. Mr Wilson was an officer. There would be no murder done on the *Leander*. If Mr Wilson were accused of murder, he would stand trial at Cork Assizes. No sooner had he said it than he knew that Best had the same thought as himself: that he, Captain Somerville, had not shown much respect for courts of law before this. But neither of them said anything. Best, though, had a bit of a twinkle in his eye when he spoke next.

'The trouble is to get Dónal and his uncle safely off the ship in Cove . . . '

'His uncle, by God! This is turning into a damned rebellion in its own right. Leave his uncle out of it, sir!'

'Begging your pardon, Captain, but the boy Dónal won't leave without his uncle. He has said so. Sullivan here will witness it.'

Captain Somerville was beginning to see that he had been outmanoeuvred by his men. 'Carry on.'

Wilson and Somerville were not on good terms but they tolerated each other for the few days of the voyage to Cork. Despite the obvious disapproval of his captain, Wilson was in rare spirits. The men observed this with considerable satisfaction. They knew what he did not, that his revenge on Dónal had failed and that his murder would soon come back to haunt him. They watched him as he hummed a tune while pacing the deck or going down to eat in the wardroom, and they knew that soon enough his world would fall on his head. Never was Thaddeus Gallahoo's song about Wilson so often called for. Wilson knew by the way it was sung that it could not be complimentary, though for the life of him he could not understand a word of the barbaric language that half of each verse was made in.

But not knowing any of what the crew knew, when Captain Somerville said he wished to speak to him, Mr Wilson went down to the interview with the clear feeling that he had the upper hand. He rather pitied plodding old Captain Somerville – but not enough to want to stay as his first officer. No, indeed. We would leave this ship with the greatest speed at Cove. He was certain of finding another, better, bigger, more important posting. All in all, Mr Wilson was very satisfied with the way he had conducted his business.

Captain Somerville did not look as if he were depressed at the thought of losing so good an officer. In fact, to Wilson's eyes, he looked decidedly contented, if not happy. He looked up from the papers he was writing and motioned Wilson to sit down, a thing he had rarely done before.

'Ah, Mr Wilson? Glorious sailing, what?' Wilson agreed, frostily, that it was indeed fine sailing weather. 'Just the thing to clear the mind, as I said to you. Put all the troubles of the shore behind you, what?' Wilson did not reply to that. He had no intention of putting anything behind him, and if the captain was seeking an apology he was wasting his time.

'I do not think, sir, that you asked me in to pass remarks on the weather.'

'Quite right, Wilson my boy. Quite right.' The 'my boy' irritated Wilson beyond belief; it was a phrase the captain generally used only with the crew.

'You are quite right, my boy. Now as it happens I am about to put the seal on my report concerning the murder of the bosun Madden, poor man. Nasty bit of business that, what?' Wilson agreed that it was indeed a nasty business.

'Quite right, my boy. And if I may say so, things look black for you. You don't come out of it well.'

Wilson was alert at once and desperately searching his mind for any mistake he might have made. He was acutely aware of the captain's self-confidence.

'I see I have startled you,' said Captain Somerville, leaning back in his chair.

Wilson tried to stay calm. He told himself that he was infinitely superior to this blundering Irishman, whose family were no more than glorified farmers from the west Cork wilderness, whose barren rocks and islands they had passed so often on this cruise. 'I am puzzled as to how I am involved, sir, that is all.'

'Come, come Wilson. This won't do, you know. Let me see.' Somerville picked up a page from the pile of papers he had before him. 'I am reading from the evidence, you understand. "The man informed me that he had been paid by a Lieutenant Wilson of the *Leander* to do violence upon a bosun of the name of Madden who would be sent by said Lieutenant to a certain place in Lady Lane in this City. There we were to fall upon him etc." Now if that ain't black, Mr Wilson, what is? The man, of course, is an utterly contemptible person. Never trust a cut-throat, Mr Wilson. It is bad policy. One of my men had this information directly from him.'

Wilson spluttered. 'But . . . but you have only the word, the word of that same cut-throat . . . '

'Don't talk rubbish on my ship, Mr Wilson, I am not accustomed to it. The man, if that is what we can call him, has been bought and paid for, sir. Bought and paid for. He has turned King's evidence. He will send you to the gallows in Cork Gaol. A most unsatisfactory end to a naval career. I don't believe I have ever met an officer who was hanged in Cork Gaol!' Captain Somerville chuckled quietly at his own joke.

Wilson tried to remain dignified, but tears of self-pity and frustration were beginning to bubble up. 'Captain, please, you will destroy me. Please . . . '

'Worse than that, Mr Wilson. Worse than that. However, I am prepared to offer you what might be called a bargain.'

He fiddled with his papers for a moment. Then, clearing his throat, he explained the bargain, counting each part out on the fingers of his left hand.

'The following events may seem unconnected to you, sir, but I assure you they are not. Take note. Firstly, a certain prisoner of the name Michael Long, through his own hand, will seem to fall over the side before we reach Cork. Best will witness it and nothing more will be heard of this prisoner. He is in chains, you see, and could be expected to sink rather quickly. You will enter his loss in the ship's log as suicide. Secondly, the ship's log contains no reference to the business with the powder monkey Dónal Long. By some strange turn of events, the boy is still aboard this boat. I call that a miracle. According to my ship's log he reported for muster in his division this morning. You will recall that it was I who took the reports this morning. Now, thirdly, as soon as we arrive at Cove, that boy's honourable discharge will be signed by you, and you and I will each present him with a letter of recommendation should he decide to go to sea again. The boy found himself here by accident and he has behaved with courage and decency. Our letter of recommendation will aid his career considerably.' The Captain paused. Wilson knew he was not finished and feared what was to come next.

'Lastly, you will sign an agreement not to pursue your career in the navy.'

Wilson stood up. 'Give up the navy, sir? Never!'

'Indeed, Mr Wilson, you will sign, or if I may say so, the Navy will give you up instead. The navy has made a point of not appointing dead men to the rank of officer.' Again he chuckled at his joke.

Wilson could see the game was up. He sat down again, slumped forward. 'You have destroyed me. Outside the navy I have no hope.'

'I have told you already you would not make a good officer. You underestimate my power and influence if you think the Admiralty would ignore my description of you. You have no future in the navy, sir. There is no new ship waiting for you at Cove. I will tell you one more thing, Mr Wilson. One more thing that you did not learn as an officer, but that you should have learned. The men will forgive a great deal in an officer. They will forgive drunkenness, foul language, meanness, lying, cheating and many other things. But they will not forgive bad seamanship or cruelty. You are guilty of both. Furthermore, let me assure you, should you continue in the navy you will one day slip on a wet deck and fall into the sea. No one will ever know whether you were pushed or not. I have seen it happen. The men will not forgive what you have done. As you value your life, leave the navy.'

'How did the boy escape?'

'Escape? I have just now explained to you that he is aboard this boat. According to the ship's log he has never left it. It is all in the log, sir. And the ship's log, you know, is the law around here.'

Mr Wilson groaned loudly. 'I will sign anything you want.'

LAST DAYS ON THE *LEANDER*

Michael Long did not see the amusing side of his supposed suicide. In great glee Captain Somerville had shown him the entry in the ship's log recording his death:

LOG OF HIS MAJESTY'S SHIP *LEANDER*	
Sept. 29th Eight miles sth. Mine Head. Sea moderate. Wind light. All sail set. Course West North-West by West. Four knots.	*At about 2 bells in the afternoon watch Gunner of the lwr deck Best reported seeing prisoner Michael Long standing in the lwr mainmast shrouds, larboard side. Said prisoner seen to make sign of cross and heard to say something in Gaelic. Said prisoner leapt into sea before said gunr Best could reach him. Cry of 'Man Overboard' raised at once. Lt. Wilson launched boat promptly, but prisoner was not seen again, perhaps due to great weight of chains on hands and feet. Verdict of suicide recorded here and attested to by me, Captain Henry Coyle Somerville R.N. and by Lieutenant Tobias Wilson R.N.'*

Captain Somerville regarded the log entry as 'a capital work of literature' and declared his intention of writing a 'storybook' on his next voyage. He had Michael Long brought out of the hold where the other prisoners were kept and ordered John Fly the ship's carpenter to strike off the chains. 'I would put you down as cook, Long, except that we already have a cook with only one hand, and even if he had two he could not cook as badly as he does now! In the meantime you may pass the remaining hours on board my ship as a passenger. For look you, that is Roche's Point on the starboard bow. We shall come up with it within this two hours if the breeze holds in this quarter. So make you ready, sir, for by nightfall you shall be ashore in Ireland again, a free man.'

Michael Long protested to Dónal that he would never commit suicide as he accounted it a terrible sin. It was a great shame to him that if he was to be written out of the world he would have to go in that way. The sailors made fun of this by telling him that he would find things a lot better at the bottom of the sea than he would in Australia. Some of them had visited that new continent and could tell the most horrific stories about monsters that lived in the wilderness, about huge deserts and terrible sea creatures that swallowed whole ships. The settlers of Australia, they said, were a cruel lot, worse than the Americans and worse than any hard-driving first officer. It would not be good to fall into their hands.

Michael Long told Dónal his story: how after Dónal had gone he had himself left home in a fit of anger; how he had gone to Wexford and been in time only for the end of the rebellion. He had not been at the Battle of Vinegar

Hill but had gone there to try to make contact with the
rest of the rebels. How he and a small group of United
Irishmen had decided to make their way northwards to
join what was left of the fighting. He had been arrested
after a skirmish with the yeomen and had been brought
to Geneva Barracks. There they had tortured him, broken
his fingers and blinded one eye. He was proud to say that
what little information he had had not been extracted
from him.

'How did you know I was on the *Leander*?'

'I got word from one of the men you met in that
tavern. A man called Edward Roche, a decent man. He
came aboard the prison ship to visit his brother and told
me you were not dead but aboard the English ship. He
was a rich gentleman, you know, so he could visit his
brother.'

Dónal remembered. 'He came aboard the *Leander* too.
In Waterford.'

'The very man. Did you not recall him from the tavern?
He was the man who spoke to your friend there. He has
done his best for us since we were captured.'

Once Michael Long said, 'I'll never be able to make up
to you for what I did before, Dónal. But I'll not let you
down again.'

Dónal made a silent vow that he would never have to
test that, never let himself sink so low that he would have
to depend on the help of his uncle. 'I cannot forget what
you did to me,' he said. 'For no one should have to endure
that. But let bygones be bygones, I say now. We will have
to struggle on together.'

In the few hours left to him on board ship, Dónal spent

his time going round to all his friends and thanking them for their kindness. There was no part of the ship where we was not welcome and everyone he met was proud of the scheme they had invented to help him escape. They all gave him advice.

'Don't join a navy ship, Dónal. They work you too hard.'

'Navy's the only place to be. Never join a merchant ship. You'll never get paid.'

'Don't go near them fancy Yankee ships. The mate of a Yankee ship would blow you down as soon as look at you. Great floggers is the mates of Yankee ships.'

'Take a voyage to China, Dónal. That's how I made me fortune.' This from one of the poorest, meanest men aboard the *Leander.*

Dónal smiled on all of them. There was much shaking of hands and nodding of heads. The sailors agreed among themselves that Dónal had been a good pupil, that he would make a fine sailor and maybe an officer one day, that they had taught him well and, taken all in all, were an excellent crew.

As the ship rounded the Cow and Calf Rocks under Roche's Point and faced up the huge harbour of Cork Dónal was sitting in the bow with his uncle. They saw the great forts at the entrance and could clearly make out the red coats of soldiers drilling on the hillsides. Beyond the forts a forest of masts showed them where Cove was. As the breeze pushed *Leander* in, boats struck out from the shore and pulled alongside shouting, 'Will you take a pilot' pulling away again at a word from an officer. Soon Corkbeg island and Ballymonas Bay were in view and

Dónal pointed out to the sailors their small cottage high on the hill behind.

The ship came to anchor first in Whitegate roadstead. Then word came out that she was to haul into the navy dock at Cove. By nightfall the chanting and hauling was done with and the *Leander* was comfortably nestled against the quay.

As soon as the mooring ropes were secured and the gangway out, Mr Wilson was seen departing. He went without a word, without even looking back, and scurried along the dock towards the town with a bag in his hand. He had scarcely walked a hundred yards before the cheering began. Men in every deck, working on the yards to furls sails 'Bristol fashion' as they called it, men scouring the deck clean, they all stopped and cheered and cheered until in embarrassment he dodged out of sight down an alley. Then the men went back to work.

Dónal was taken aside by Best and ship's carpenter John Fly at four bells in the first watch.

'We've found you a ship, Dónal,' John Fly told him. 'A Yankee brig. What do you think, she's the very brig we searched a few months back.'

'I've spoke to the skipper for you, Dónal, and he remembers you well. He says he'll take you on as cabin boy. And since he don't have a cook, he'll take your uncle on too. Being half-blind and having only one hand is no trouble to a cook.'

'Why, I've never knowed a cook 'ad all 'is 'ands and legs,' John Fly said with some indignation. 'If 'e 'ad, he'd be a sailor, not a cook.'

Dónal could not thank them enough.

'All we asks,' said John Fly, a tear in his eye, 'is that you remembers poor John Fly an' Best an' all yer mates when some day yer on the quarterdeck. Cast an eye on the old *Leander* some day as you pass by in a cloud o'glory, and hail yer old shipmates. Just for old time's sake.' Here he began to cry openly, pulling out a dirty yellow piece of cloth from the pocket of his breeches and blowing his nose loudly into it at the same time.

'None of your blubbering, John Fly. It ain't fitting in a man of your rank. Ship's carpenter, no less. I wouldn't expect it of a powder monkey!' John Fly could not contain his grief and left them, waving a hand behind him as he went.

Thaddeus Gallahoo came up then and presented Dónal with a sheet of rough paper on which he had pains-takingly written out the song about their battle with the Frenchman. The writing was cramped and irregular and the spelling was terrible, but Dónal knew it represented two or three hours' work for the shantyman. He looked at the words and at Thaddeus Gallahoo and said he would learn them and sing them in every ship he sailed in so that the name of Thaddeus Gallahoo would be remembered all over the world. The shantyman looked embarrassed and downcast until Dónal said, 'Sure it's only fitting for a prince of the Gallahoos to be a writer of songs and have them sung everywhere.' The shantyman brightened then and warmly shook Dónal's hand. 'I'll see you in port,' he said, 'wherever that might be.'

Best and John Fly had not only found him a ship but had taken up a collection among the men, a collection which had turned out a tarry hat and jacket better than the ones he had and not much bigger, a muffler to warm his throat on the long night watches, eighteen pence in various coins, a sailor's clasp knife, a woolly jumper, a pair of worsted stockings, a piece of ribbon for when Dónal's hair was long enough to plait into a pigtail, a piece of whalebone with a ship carved on it and the date 1782, and a cloth bag; all of which were presented to him in a battered old sea chest. Dónal realised that these were the treasures of poor seamen who could ill-afford to part with any of them. The sea chest had formerly been used in the ship's carpenter's store for holding odds and ends, but now he saw his own name painted in white on its side – *Dónal Long*. Sailors are very proud and careful of their chests. In some ways the sea chest is the sailor's home. It is the only thing that follows him from ship to ship, containing everything he owns. No decent sailor would be without one. Dónal finally felt as if he belonged, just when he was leaving.

The presentation was made in the middle deck, by the light of the battle lanterns, and Captain Somerville was invited. When the men had given Dónal their gifts and he had thanked them, the captain stepped forward. Into Dónal's hand he placed a battered book.

'*The Principles of Navigation*, Dónal. Study them and I declare you will rise in the world. You won't have to steal a fishing smack to be master of her. You'll master a fine ship one day. I hope it may be in this navy.' All the men approved heartily and loudly of this. 'A speech!' they cried. 'A word from Dónal!' So Dónal made a small speech.

'My friends, and Captain, I did not choose to come aboard the *Leander*, as you know.' (Chuckles all round.)

'But my own ship had made up her mind to give up sailing.' (Loud laughter.) 'I did not expect, when I came aboard, to find so many true and loyal friends. I promise, as I live, Dónal Long will not forget you. If I ever do rise and become a captain, which with this book I might do, I swear to fill my ship with brandy and every man-jack of you may drink it dry!' By the end of this speech the between-decks was resounding with cheering and hooting. Dónal was hoisted up so that he banged his head off the ceiling, then passed from hand to hand, each person clapping him upon the back. When the time came to leave he had to struggle to escape, and as he climbed the ladder to the upper deck he saw that the sailors had formed a circle and Thaddeus Gallahoo was singing the song of 'Captain Somerville and the Frenchman'. Captain Somerville himself looked on, beaming, and the battle-lantern threw its yellow light on every honest face.

In this circle of friends, joined by a song, Dónal saw the only protection he had ever enjoyed in his life. He wondered that the circle of peace and friendship should be the crew of a fighting ship of war, dedicated to the destruction of an enemy.

Now that they were practically ashore, the rhythm of shipboard life, punctuated by bells and watches, seemed to be disrupted. At about midnight, Dónal and his uncle stepped down the dark gangway and on to the quay. Best helped Dónal to carry his sea chest to the part of town known as the Holy Ground. This was where the worst taverns were, and where merchant ships, especially American merchant ships, preferred to tie up. There Dónal saw the Yankee brig for the second time. He turned to Best and warmly shook his hand.

'Farewell old friend. I'll see you again some time I hope.'

'Fair weather, Dónal.' And Best was gone, weaving through the crowd that swept along the waterfront.

Dónal looked around him but could recognise nothing that he might take with him as a memory of home. Even the accents were not Irish but Russian, American, English, Scottish, Spanish, Dutch – people of every nationality jabbering away as if this waterfront were their own home port and this night was the finest, warmest, happiest night they had ever lived through. The skirl of a fiddle, the hoarse voice of some shantyman singing a shoreside song, the shouted chorus – these were the sounds he would carry with him and he knew in his heart that he would hear them for ever more, those same sounds, in every seaport and harbour quay of his future life.

So he hoisted his sea chest onto his shoulders, his possessions rattling inside, and, followed by his uncle, he strode up the gangway of the American brig, *Provident of Boston*. He was bound for the New World.